He placed his arm walked to the side through the darkn frightened girl.

'Thou art a witch, t All my prayers an drive Satan from thee. You are beyond help.' As he spoke, his hand reached around behind the brass headboard. The girl felt the rope tightening around her neck. She tried to scream, but nothing came out. Her pale white body arched and twisted as she struggled. Her tongue shot out of her mouth and lolled from side to side. Her blue eyes bulged. Finally, she lay motionless.

JACK CANNON

The Hammer of God

Grafton Books

A Division of HarperCollins*Publishers*

GraftonBooks
A Division of HarperCollins*Publishers*
77–85 Fulham Palace Road,
Hammersmith, London W6 8JB

A Grafton UK Paperback Original 1991
9 8 7 6 5 4 3 2 1

ISBN 0-586-20457-1

Printed and bound in Great Britain by
Collins, Glasgow

*NOTE TO THE READER

The Hammer of God was first published in October, 1974, by Nordon Publications/Leisure Books and was written by Nelson De Mille. Jack Cannon is a pseudonym for Nelson De Mille.

The Hammer of God is part of a series of six previously published books now published by Grafton Books under their original titles. They were originally published in the USA as follows:

The Sniper	Nordon Publications/ Leisure Books	August, 1974
The Hammer of God	Nordon Publications/ Leisure Books	October, 1974
The Smack Man	Manor Books	March, 1975
The Cannibal	Manor Books	April, 1975
The Night of the Phoenix	Manor Books	June, 1975
The Death Squad	Manor Books	August, 1975

Each of these books has been revised and updated by the author. In the Nordon Publications/Leisure Books editions, the main character was Detective Joe Ryker. In the Manor Books editions, the main character was Detective Joe Keller. For continuity, all of the new Grafton editions use the name of Joe Ryker for the main character.

We hope that the original fans of Detective Joe Ryker and Detective Joe Keller, as well as new readers, will enjoy these updated and revised books.

THE HAMMER
OF GOD

ONE

The big man sat upright, a look of horror on his face. It was as bad as he had thought it would be, filled with sound, fury, lightning, fog, and blasphemy.

On stage, three witches cackled and shrieked and cavorted in lewd, suggestive ways. They mocked God with their very presence.

The man clenched his fists and ground his teeth as he watched with sickened fascination. Unbelievably, everybody else in the audience remained calm in the face of Evil.

When he could stand it no longer, he ran from the theater, his stomach heaving, his heavy brows creased with dread.

Outside, in the cold December air, his terror turned to wrath. He grabbed the cowl of his black monk's robe and flipped it over his head. He was prepared.

He stood under the marquee of the small theater and stared at the passing traffic. His coal-black eyes burned red in the reflected glare of the city lights. For the next hour, he waited motionless, his lips moving in prayer. Above his head, the sign on the marquee read: MACBETH.

The crowded theater had emptied and the theater-goers had given the large man only a passing glance as they filed out. A robed monk wasn't the strangest sight New Yorkers saw on the streets.

The monk, Zachariah, picked up a black canvas bag at his feet and slung it over his shoulder. He thrust his big hands into the coarse woolen folds of his robe and began walking. Large silent snowflakes began falling as he walked past the blazing Christmas displays on Fourteenth Street in Manhattan.

"Pagan lights in the city of the pagans," he muttered. "My work will begin here."

Snowflakes lighted on the high bridge of his hawk-like nose and nestled in his full black beard. As he walked, white mist rose from his mouth and nostrils. His lips moved quickly and silently, as if in prayer.

He stopped abruptly before the small theater's backstage door and waited. In the distance, over the muffled sounds of traffic, the clock in the Con Ed tower began to chime midnight. Suddenly the stage door swung open. Zachariah stepped into the shadows. The actors and actresses filed out in small groups. Making appropriate comments about the falling snow, they began to scatter, but the play's three witches stood together. One of them threw back her head and said, "When will we three meet again? In thunder, lightning, or in rain?"

The second witch gave the response: "When the hurlyburly's done, when the battle's lost and won."

They laughed at their play-acting. They did this every night. The last of the chimes died away.

Macbeth moved over to the three witches. "Let me

walk you home," he said to the third and prettiest one.

The girl smiled and shook her head. As she turned and walked off, a gust of wind caught her black cape and it billowed out behind her. Zachariah half expected her to lift off the ground and fly into the full moon. Instead, she walked with long, graceful strides down the dark side street; her black leather knee boots gleamed as she passed a lamp pole.

The robed man waited in the shadow. Then he began to follow the witch.

As she moved out of the small puddle of light cast by the street lamp, she vanished. Zachariah thought she had disappeared forever, but she reappeared after a minute under the next street lamp. He breathed more easily and picked up his pace.

They walked on Fourteenth for a few minutes, the street becoming darker and quieter the further east they traveled. Zachariah closed the gap slowly with every minute. The girl turned south on First Avenue for a few blocks, then bounded up the steps of an old five-story walk-up apartment house. Her frozen fingers fumbled furiously with her keys. She had no doubt now that she was being followed. Suddenly, she felt wetness around her mouth and nose. A sweet, cloying odor rose in her nostrils. Then blackness.

She opened her eyes slowly and looked around. Her senses began returning slowly. She could see a tall white candle burning above her feet. Otherwise the room was in darkness. She could smell, through the lingering sweetness in her nostrils, the acrid fumes of burning incense. She could feel that she was lying on a bed and that she was naked. She could hear a man's voice chanting behind her. Then she tasted the rising

bile and vomit in her throat, brought on by the
chloroform.

The pretty witch sobbed and tried to get up, but a
sharp pain around her throat jerked her head back.
She lay still for a moment, trying to fight the nausea.
When her head had cleared, she realized that she was
spread-eagled, tied by her wrists and ankles to the
bedposts. She panicked and began twisting against her
bonds. Finally, she could hold back the sickness no
longer. She vomited and the vomit spread across her
face; she swallowed some of it and began choking. She
spat and twisted and gagged and vomited for five
minutes. Her face was white. Tears formed in her eyes
and her nose ran as she fought for air. At length, she
lay back, exhausted. Her breath began to return with
steady heaves of her chest. All the while, through her
agony, she could hear the steady hoarse chanting
behind her head. The phone was ringing.

The weak light of the long taper was blurry through
her tears. She lay still for a moment and tried to
collect her thoughts. The low chanting suddenly
stopped. She could hear a heavy book close. The
phone stopped ringing.

"Help me," she whimpered.

No answer.

"Help me, please. Who are you?" She began crying,
softly.

"For the last hour I have been trying to help you,"
came a deep, low voice. "But you are beyond help."

The girl suddenly wondered if she were in a hospital, if she were sick or dying. But the bed . . . the wall
near her head . . . this was her apartment.

"I'm all right now," she said, timidly. "Untie me,
please."

"Lying she-devil! Obscene witch!" His voice
cracked with anger. "Do you really think you can fool
me so easily?"

12

Witch? The girl suddenly understood. This was insane. In her mind she vacillated between anger and pleading. Finally she said firmly, "Look here, I only *play* the part of a witch. This is silly. Please untie me and let me get dressed—I'm freezing."

The voice behind her boomed again. "What! You dare make demands of God's Avenger?"

"Please."

"You are a filthy witch and you have no shame, so I will not cover you. It is cold in this room because of your unholy presence, you unspeakable obscenity. You are beyond help."

The girl lay still. She tried to make believe she was dreaming. She wondered if this was some sort of bad joke being played on her by her fellow actors. In a minute the lights would go on and the room would be filled with laughing friends.

"Martin. Martin. Is that you? This isn't funny. . . ."

"Silence! Do not call on any of your spirits for help."

The voice was threatening—too threatening. No one she knew could act that well. No, this was not a joke. The young actress began shivering.

"Stop that infernal quaking," the voice boomed.

"I'm freezing," she whispered. "Please let me go."

"You are possessed of Satan, unholy witch. That is why you vomit and twist and shake. These are not the illnesses of a mortal body. These are the signs of your possession."

She shook her head as best she could. "No. No," she said, desperately. "The ether—the chloroform—whatever—made me sick. It's cold. I'm freezing. I'm not a witch."

She suddenly realized how absurd she sounded. What type of lunacy was this? Why did she have to beg and defend herself against charges of witchcraft?

13

She became angry and screamed, "Let me go! Untie me! Get out—" Her voice was choked off with a twist of the rope around her neck. The phone began ringing again.

From behind her, Zachariah twisted and tightened the garrote. The girl passed out.

Zachariah walked around to the foot of the bed and stared down at the naked girl from behind the burning candle. His red-rimmed eyes glowed and danced in the reflected flame.

Presently, she opened her eyes and began raising her head slowly. The rope around her neck was slack. She looked down her body, past her feet and beyond the candle. She gasped as she saw the tall, hooded figure staring at her. He raised his right hand and pointed an accusing finger.

"Thou art a witch," he said in a low, threatening voice.

She broke out in a cold sweat. "No."

"Thou art a shameless witch."

Zachariah thrust his left hand into the folds of his monk's robe, then, still pointing the accusing finger at her, he drew out a stiff parchment and began reading.

"How long have you been a witch?"

Silence.

"Why did you become a witch?"

Silence.

"What is the name of your master among the evil demons? Did you have intercourse with your evil master? With Satan?"

Intercourse? Suddenly she had hope. This was a madman, but he was a man.

"Yes. Let's have intercourse. Make love to me. Untie me and let's do it."

"What!" The monk's voice rose to a near shriek. "You filthy creature of hell!"

She had made a serious miscalculation and she knew it. Zachariah hurried through the rest of the required questioning.

"Where is your unholy Sabbat held? What injuries have you done? What spells have you cast? Who are your accomplices? . . ."

"No!" she shrieked. "You're insane. Get out. . . ."

"Silence!" roared the hooded figure.

He placed his arms in the folds of his robe and walked to the side of the bed. His eyes glowed in the flickering candlelight as he bent over the naked, frightened girl.

"Thou art a witch, though thou refuses to confess. All my prayers and all my exorcisms have failed to drive Satan from thee. You are beyond help," he said in funereal tones.

As he spoke, he reached around behind the brass headboard; the girl felt the rope tightening around her neck. She tried to scream, but nothing came out. Her pale white body arched and twisted as she struggled; her tongue lolled from the side of her mouth. Her pretty blue eyes bulged. Finally, she lay motionless.

Zachariah pulled a long silver dagger from his robe and placed the point at the base of the dead girl's throat and pressed until the skin broke. He moved the knife slowly downward over her breastbone, between her full breasts, down her belly and over her navel. He stopped at her forest of pubic hair. A long red line followed the point of the knife. Then with one motion Zachariah slashed the top of her breasts from armpit to armpit. He put the bloody dagger on her belly and drew a wooden stake and mallet from his shoulder bag. He placed the point of the stake over the girl's heart at the intersection of the bloody cross he had carved into her body. With one massive swing of the mallet, he drove the stake through the breastbone and into the still heart. The second blow drove the stake out her back and into the soft mattress. A final blow pushed the stake flush with her bloody flesh. The hammer cracked three ribs.

Zachariah straightened up, said the Prayer of the Dead over her body, gathered up his belongings and left.

TWO

Five blocks from where the witch died in agony, Detective Sergeant Joe Ryker walked slowly toward the Eighth Precinct. Last night's snow had turned to dirty slush by midday and was now forming into gray ice as the sun began to sink; it cracked and broke under the big cop's feet as he pushed against the icy wind.

Ryker wasn't wearing an overcoat because he had forgotten to pick it up at the Chink laundry. He had had other things on his mind for the past three weeks. In fact, he had been fighting to save his ass from the police bureaucracy, that monolith of rules and regulations tied with red tape. He didn't know if he had won, but he was back on the job at least temporarily. Without the job, Ryker didn't exist.

A few minutes later he mounted the worn stone steps of the dilapidated Eighth Precinct house, and walked quickly through the institutional green lobby, past the desk sergeant and up the staircase.

The detectives' squad room looked seedier than ever this afternoon. Some well-intentioned asshole

had hung Christmas decorations from the new fluo-
rescent light fixtures. The effect was to make the high
zinc-ceilinged room look gloomier than ever in con-
trast to the sparkling tin-foil stars, angels, and bells.

Ryker grumbled as he looked around. Sergeant Bo
Lindly stood up and walked over to Ryker.

"Welcome back and merry Christmas, Joe. How do
you like our handiwork this year?" He smiled as he
waved his hand around the room.

"Looks like a fucking kindergarten," Ryker said,
walking to his desk and sitting down.

Lindly followed. "You're not big on Christmas, I
see."

"Fuck Christmas," Ryker said. "This is supposed to
be a police station, not a fucking funny farm where the
inmates cut out stars and bells."

Lindly was annoyed. He wanted to cheer Ryker up
after all the man had been through. He stared at Ryker
for a second. Ryker's sharp green eyes met Lindly's.
Lindly had to turn away. You had to be careful with
Ryker.

"Okay, Scrooge," Lindly said. "Then maybe we
have something to improve your Christmas spirit. A
girl got butchered in her apartment on East Eleventh
Street. Lieutenant Fischetti caught the squeal."

Ryker lifted his bulk from the creaky swivel chair
and crossed the long squad room. He went into the
cubicle that was Lieutenant Fischetti's office and sat
down.

Fischetti cringed. He never knew how to handle this
strange man. He outranked Ryker, but still, he was
uneasy in his presence. At last he cleared his throat.
"Welcome back," he said, trying to be friendly.

"Can it, Loo," Ryker said. "You don't give a shit
one way or the other."

Fischetti started to say something, then thought

18

better of it. He really *didn't* care about Ryker—except that the man knew too much about his, Fischetti's, role in the sniper case. Fischetti still felt guilty about letting Ryker down, almost getting him killed with his lack of support.

"I guess the IAD boys are satisfied," Fischetti said, referring to the Internal Affairs Division.

"Shooflies eat shit," Ryker said, tiring of the preliminaries. "I'm back on duty and that's all you need to know. You got something for me or not?"

"Are you feeling up to it? I mean physically? You can push some papers for awhile, if you want," Fischetti said. The thought of Ryker back on the street made him nervous.

"Shoulder's fine," Ryker said. He had taken a .45 slug in the shoulder, a gift from Henry Cyrus, the sniper. It still hurt like hell, but Ryker would never admit it. He would also never admit his own part in the sniper's death. When they had found Cyrus frozen solid on a Long Island City rooftop, handcuffed, his teeth knocked out, everyone knew Ryker had done it. But nobody could prove it. And after three weeks, nobody *wanted* to prove it. There were too many high-powered politicians, police brass, and federal agents mixed up in the case. The last thing they wanted was to give Ryker a forum. They wanted him dead or silent; that's why he was back at the precinct where they knew he'd keep his mouth shut.

Such were the politics of police science, Fischetti thought. "Okay, then. We just caught a homicide on East Eleventh. Everybody's there already."

"Right," Ryker said, getting up and leaving.

Fischetti was disappointed. In the movies this was always a dramatic scene where the boss, sitting in a big office, gives the details of the case to his top man. The lieutenant looked around. His wasn't much of an office. He wasn't really the boss—Deputy Inspector Connolly would be, and Ryker, although maybe his top man, didn't seem too interested in the details.

When Ryker had gone, Fischetti stared down at his desk and wondered why he couldn't give a briefing like they did in the movies.

Outside the station house, Ryker turned north on Avenue A and walked through the gathering darkness. He passed by the strange world of the East Village without looking up. Freezing prostitutes stood in doorways looking sadder than usual. Potential muggers and burglars drank in bars waiting for nightfall. Junkies and pushers met, shook hands, and separated. The invading yuppies in their Paul Stuart overcoats hurried to their converted brownstones, content to light a fire in their wbfp's and thank their stars they had the acumen to buy before the prices skyrocketed. Crack houses and lawyers' houses stood side by side, the occupants of both making a nice living off the misery of others.

The contrasts in this neighborhood were so striking that an out-of-town policeman once said to Ryker, "Don't New Yorkers know how to separate themselves into classes? How can all these different people exist like this, side by side?"

Ryker never gave it much thought. It seemed to him that everyone, out-of-towners and native New Yorkers alike, talked for hours about this city and its problems. He, Ryker, within his own small area of responsibility, did something about it. Over the years he had brought countless felons to court. Not necessarily to justice, but to court. The ones he had brought to justice were the ten he had killed over the years.

Homicide was his life's blood. The investigation of the violent deaths of his fellow citizens, so much a natural part of any big city, was how he earned his money. It was the only thing that even remotely interested him. How, why, when, and where human beings terminated the lives of other human beings was the only subject that he would talk about, when he talked at all.

Ryker walked quickly until he reached Eleventh Street, then he turned right and spotted the police cars and vans halfway down the bleak block. Despite the cold, the promise of seeing a dead body had drawn thirty or forty rubberneckers. Ryker pinned his gold shield to his dark brown winter suit, his ticket of admission to all crime scenes.

He passed through the police barricades and mounted the crumbling steps of the apartment house. On the stoop, a young patrolman was standing in a modified position of parade rest. He saw Ryker's gold shield and brought his legs together, at the same time touching the bill of his cap with a gloved hand. Ryker passed by and moved into the small foyer. A few uniformed patrolmen eyed him uneasily as he lit a cigar. Ryker's face and reputation were known all over the city, and there was some talk that a lot of uniforms had died for his sins. The two young cops suddenly wished that they had something to do, but their sergeant had told them to "just stand there and look busy."

Ryker approached them. He knew that there were always too many uniforms around after a homicide was committed. It was a waste of manpower, but the brass seemed to feel that the public expected a lot of blue after a murder—especially if there were none around before.

Ryker stared at the men. "What's your function?"

The young men looked panicky. One of them saved the situation by blurting, "Just trying to look busy as ordered, sir."

Ryker almost smiled. "You're doing a piss-poor job of it. Give me a quick run-down." He pointed upstairs where police-type noises were wafting down the stairwell.

"Yes, sir." One of them began. "Young, pretty—name of Tami Long, a bit actress. Came home from a gig at the St. Mark Theatre last night. Didn't show up at rehearsal this afternoon. About two o'clock the director calls the station house and asks if we can send a car over to check her out. Apparently the girl was never late for rehearsal before and so forth. Nobody answered the phone. Patrolman named Walinsky got the passkey from the super and went in." The cop swallowed.

"You been upstairs yet?"

"Yes, sir."

"Get on with it, then."

The young cop continued and described as best he could what he had seen. Ryker turned away after he had finished and began mounting the creaky stairs. He always got background from a patrolman before he ran into his fellow detectives and the brass. It gave him an idea of what to expect, what to ask, and what to answer when he got to the actual scene. Usually, however, he looked for a veteran cop to squeeze, but the frigid weather had driven the smart ones indoors.

Ryker reached the fourth-floor landing and looked around. The small hallway was jammed with detectives, veteran patrolmen, forensic people, and newsmen. Ryker looked into the open doorway across the hall. The bed was in his line of sight, and he could see the naked girl with her legs spread open as if she were waiting for a lover to break away from the milling crowd of men and come to her. Her arms, too, were spread above her head.

Ryker moved closer, then passed by a burly patrolman, signed the crime-scene log, received his plastic gloves and shoe covers, and stepped into the apartment. A few newsmen tried to follow, but were held back. The four detectives in the room nodded to him. Ryker stared at the naked figure for a moment. The corpse's breasts were big and white; the aureoles and nipples were small and just as pale as the breasts. In fact her whole body was drained of color, except her face, which was lobster red. Her tongue stuck out as though she were mocking all the men around her bed.

Ryker could see that her buttocks were red where the blood had settled after death; the blue eyes were wide open; the white skin was flawless except for the obvious cross cut into her flesh and the tip of the stake through her heart. The blood had coagulated and turned brown.

Ryker looked at her face again. Despite the vomit-streaked mouth and chin, he knew he was looking at a very pretty girl. Her long black hair formed a frame between her red face and the white sheets. The soles of her feet were black. She must have walked barefoot a lot.

Ryker studied the rope around her neck. Death by strangulation, he concluded. Mouth open, eyes open. If that stake passed through her heart while it was beating, there would have been blood splattered all over the place. The cross was carved on her body after death, too, he thought.

He took in the rest of the death scene, then turned around. The corpse had nothing left to offer him. A dozen men worked silently in the cramped one-room apartment. Detectives were going through her closet, her dresser, her small bathroom, and her meager possessions. Two men from Forensic were picking up hairs, fingernail clippings, and incidentals with a tweezer and magnifying glass. A police photographer excused himself, moved around Ryker, and began taking pictures of her. The assistant medical examiner asked for close-ups. The obliging photographer bent over and took pictures of her left breast, her right breast, her face, her hands, her feet, her pubic region. He took dozens of small disjointed pictures, each time laying a six-inch ruler next to the area being photographed. The invasion of the girl's privacy was complete.

A group of newsmen again tried to get in when they saw the flashbulbs popping, but the big cop at the door held up his hand. This was still admission by shield only.

The two forensic men left with their hand vacuum cleaner and glassine envelopes filled with bits and pieces.

Ryker noticed the guttered candle had melted onto the brass footboard of the bed; the girl's clothes lay in an inverted ball at his feet. She didn't undress herself, he decided.

He looked again between the girl's shapely legs. A white string hung loosely from between her labia. A tampon. No penetration, he thought. His mind was working, but he was coming up blank. Rape, followed by murder, was common enough. Murder, then rape, was not as common. Stripping, binding, and murder without rape was an unusual event. Maybe her period stopped him? Not likely, he thought. He had a feeling this was going to be a tough one. Worse yet, it looked methodical, diabolical. This was not an act of passion, but a conscious act of destruction. There might be more.

Chief of Detectives Timothy Lockman arrived with a small entourage. He spotted Ryker and took two big steps toward him.

"You in on this, Ryker?"

24

"I suppose so," Ryker said.

"I'm putting Deputy Inspector Connolly in charge of the task force. Give him a hand," Lockman said and left with his men.

"Right," Ryker said, wishing *he* was in charge. But that's the way things were these days. A small-time murder went to the PDU, the Precinct Detective Unit. That usually meant Ryker and his ineffectual boss, Lieutenant Fischetti. But when a respectable citizen got iced or some maniac was on the loose, policy dictated a city-wide task force with at least a captain in charge.

Ryker had worked for Captain Carl Peterson on three task forces, the last being the sniper manhunt. Peterson had fucked him, but had, in turn, been fucked by George McVey, the former chief of detectives, who, in turn, was eighty-sixed by the outgoing P.C. Heads were still rolling; Ryker's was attached by a thread. Now they wanted him to work with Deputy Inspector Connolly, of all people.

The big cop at the door turned over his post to a younger patrolman and cornered Ryker.

"Remember me?" the cop said. "I'm Manion. I seen you work before—the Haitian headhunters."

"Sure," Ryker said. All big fat patrolmen looked the same to him.

"Is it true they're bringing Connolly back?" Manion asked.

"You heard the chief," Ryker said.

"But I thought he was crazy or somethin'."

"How the fuck would I know?" Ryker said.

"Story is, he went crazy cuz of you," Manion said. He smiled, revealing large, greenish-yellow teeth.

"I can't help it if everyone loves me," Ryker said. "Now close that fucking door and get rid of those vultures. You stay out there, too."

Ryker walked across the room and sat down on the bed next to the unprotesting corpse. He lit a cigar.

There were twelve people in the small room now: the four detectives from Ryker's precinct, whom he knew well, two men dusting for fingerprints, the photographer standing next to his tripod, the assistant medical examiner, the two patrolmen who had originally found the body and who were still filling out reports, himself, and the dead girl.

"Doc?" Ryker turned to the elderly M.E.

The doctor picked up his notebook and squinted at it. "Yes. All right. Death was by strangulation. That rope around her neck, obviously. Death occurred about three A.M. Under the dried vomit around her mouth, there's greenish and yellowish coloring— indicating that she was chloroformed. We'll know after the autopsy. That's what probably caused the vomiting, by the way."

The doctor went on and everyone listened silently.

"The stake through the heart did not contribute to her death. It looks like a ritual murder to me."

"That's my job," Ryker snapped. He didn't like medical people. Their overblown egos collided with his own. They could be as insufferable as he was when working on a case. The doctor had dealt with Ryker before, so he turned away and made himself seem busy.

Ryker ordered the two patrolmen to recount everything that had happened since they received the call to check out the apartment. Next, the four detectives did the same thing. As everyone spoke in turn, the two fingerprint men continued dusting. When everyone was debriefed, there was a long silence. Ryker turned halfway around and stared at the dead girl behind him. He turned back.

"So this girl walks home from the theater where she

has a bit part," he began as if to himself. "She's maybe followed. Maybe somebody is waiting in front of the building for her. Maybe he's already in the apartment. Maybe she knew the guy and let him in. Anyway, he chloroformed her. Inside the apartment, he strips her and ties her spread-eagle on the bed. She's probably still unconscious, right? From the looks of those clothes, she didn't take them off herself. No signs of struggle in the room. Everybody agree so far?"

The four detectives nodded. The other men knew Ryker wasn't talking to them and continued with what they were doing. A flashbulb popped from time to time.

"She vomits—probably from chloroform. Then the perp or perps garrote her with the rope. He cuts a cross in her body, then drives a stake through her heart in that order—right, Doc?"

"Yes," the doctor said. "The cross was cut first—then the stake."

"Why didn't this clown screw her? Fernandez?" Ryker asked.

The middle-aged Puerto Rican detective looked alert. "Yes?"

"If you chloroformed a good-looking piece like this, stripped her, and tied her spread-eagle on a bed, what would be your next move?"

Fernandez was embarrassed. He was a good family man with five kids, and for the last two hours he had been trying to avoid thoughts like this. Now Ryker had asked him to speak aloud what he had been trying to put out of his mind.

"I . . . I guess. . . "

"Is this a toughie, Fernandez?"

The cop looked distraught. "No, no, I would make love to her."

"Screw her?"

"Yes, of course."

"Is there anyone here who wouldn't? What do you think about it, Doc?"

Dr. Morlock, the assistant medical examiner, had been thinking this over and had come to a conclusion. "There has been no sexual activity here."

"How can you be so sure? Whether he screwed her in the straight way or not, there's a lot of sexual overtones to a murder where the victim is female, naked, and bound," Ryker said.

"Nothing of that sort happened here, Sergeant," the doctor said firmly.

Ryker looked at him. "You haven't examined the corpse completely. When you get Tami Long back to the morgue you may find that there was anal penetration, maybe oral. Maybe normal intercourse took place and for some perverted reason the perp replaced the tampon. He may have jerked off while he was torturing her. There's a lot of kinky sex shit to think about here."

The men stared at the corpse as though they expected her to tell them a good story. They looked toward each other; they had all known similar cases in the past. This was no surprise to any of them, but Ryker knew it had to be said again. He looked up.

"Okay. How about the candle, the cross, and the stake?"

"Ritual murder," Detective Littel said before anyone could beat him to it.

"Or maybe made to look like one for some reason," Ryker said. "What kind of ritual?"

Dr. Morlock cleared his throat. Ryker looked at him and nodded. The man began slowly.

"As was pointed out to me before, this is not my business, but I have some experience in this field, having studied the occult as a young—"

"Your Witch Doctor credentials are fine, Doc. Go ahead," Ryker said.

The doctor looked embarrassed, but said, "Well, anyway, it looks to be the exact opposite of a Satanic murder. That is, this is the way witches are—were—sometimes executed instead of burning or drowning, which was much more common.

"Strangulation or hanging was always followed by burning or driving an oaken stake through the heart. This was ostensibly to keep the victim's immortal soul at rest after the mortal killing. Burning is preferred because it precludes the necessity of a stake and is more permanent." The doctor suddenly realized he was speaking as though it were fact, not legend he was explaining.

"Please watch your tenses," Ryker said. Several men laughed uneasily. The flustered assistant medical examiner continued.

"Yes, this is a hobby of mine. As a man of science . . ."

"Get on with it."

"Well, all right, the candle. We can see that it is white. Witches use—used—black candles. Exorcists, priests, use white ones. They still do."

The elderly doctor looked around, found a wobbly folding chair, and sat down. He looked shaky. The room was stuffy and smelled of sweat, blood, and mortality. Ryker asked the two men from Fingerprints and the photographer to leave. The three men were long since finished but had tried to look busy; they didn't want to miss a good story. They looked disappointed when they left.

Fernandez filled a glass of water from the chipped sink in the kitchen alcove and handed it to Dr. Morlock. He drank, blew his nose, and continued.

"Where was I? Yes, the candle. So what we seem to

have here is the murder of a young girl suspected of witchcraft. She may very well have been a witch, too."

"What the fuck are you talking about?" Ryker asked, irritated.

"There's still plenty of witches around, Sergeant. There must be a dozen Black Masses held in this city on every Sabbat. . . ."

"Sabbath?" Detective Littel asked.

"Sabbat. Like the Sabbath. Black Mass is a parody of the Christian mass."

"Sounds like fun," Ryker said. "How do you know she was a witch?"

The doctor looked surprised. "By the way she was murdered, of course."

"That doesn't make too much fucking sense to me, Doc. If you find a guy hanged, it doesn't mean he was a horse thief. Is there anything in this room to lead you to believe the victim practiced witchcraft?"

"No—and it's strange that there isn't."

"Why?"

"Because somehow the murderer believed she was a witch."

"Who murdered her, Dr. Morlock?"

"A witch-hunter, of course. An exorcist. A priest who draws the devil out of a possessed body. If he fails, he sometimes kills the victim or has her killed. You must have seen the movie."

"What movie?"

"The Exorcist."

"I don't go to movies," Ryker said, dismissing the doctor as some kind of jerk.

"Is everyone in the building being questioned right now?"

"Affirmative," Littel answered. "All the actors from her play are at the St. Mark Theatre. Procino is handling it. I called before."

"And?"

"Well—these actor types, you know . . ."

"No."

"They're giving our boys a rough time. They're all trying to out-cool each other, I guess."

"Why doesn't Procino lean on them a little?"

"I think he's in love with all the actresses," Littel said, smiling.

"Asshole. We'll get down there and chew some butt."

There was a knock on the door. Ryker bounced off the bed and opened it. The men watched as four medical attendants filed in with a stretcher.

"Finished, Doc?" one of them asked.

"Yes. Yes. Go ahead."

The men walked over to the small bed. The room was silent as everyone suddenly became aware again of the girl. The subject of all their discussion had been almost forgotten as she lay quietly on her bed.

The attendants tried to look professional in front of the cops, but the girl was beautiful despite what had happened to her. Dead or not, it seemed strange that she should be lying naked on her bed while dozens of clothed men talked about her, poked her, photographed her, and sat down on her bed with her.

The attendants cut the four cords that bound her with a borrowed penknife. The body was stiff now, and the men had difficulty bringing her arms down across her chest. They pulled and bent, but the girl, in death, offered more resistance to four grown men than she ever could have in life. Finally, her arms were crossed over her breasts, and the men squeezed her cold, shapely legs together. They placed the stretcher on the floor beside the bed, while one man grabbed her head and another clasped her ankles; they began pulling, but the cold, clammy body refused to move.

The attendants looked around, perplexed. Everyone in the room was absolutely still; no one seemed to know what to say. The men tried again. The body was stuck.

"The stake! The stake!" The assistant medical examiner was on his feet. "The stake is stuck in the mattress."

The attendants looked at each other. *What stake?*

The oak stake was flush with the girl's chest and covered by coagulated blood. The doctor explained and the four men responded. They thrust their hands and arms under the girl's thighs, buttocks, back, neck and shoulders. She was very cold. They lifted in unison. The stake slid out of the mattress. They stepped backward across the stretcher and laid their prize on it. The long stake held in her chest and propped up her shoulders. Her neck, stiff with rigor mortis, remained straight and supported her head; her long black hair hung down onto the stretcher. She looked like she was sunbathing in the nude on a chaise longue—except that her skin was so white.

The attendants looked at Dr. Morlock.

"Forget it. Forget it," he said uneasily. "Cover her."

The men folded the four canvas covers over the upraised girl. They strapped the belts tight, and the body sank a bit under the canvas as the belts were drawn. They lifted the stretcher and left with the M.E.

The hallway began exploding with flashbulbs. Manion, the uniformed cop outside, closed the door again. Ryker walked over and examined the hole in the mattress, then turned and faced the remaining men in the room.

"Littel, what's playing at the St. Mark?"

"MacGreggor."

"What?"

"Mac—something."

Ryker picked up a small playbill from the coffee table. *"Macbeth* by William Shakespeare." He flipped through it. "Witches: Rena Williams, Cathy Tobey, and Tami Long." He stuffed the playbill in his pocket. "Let's go to the theater, Littel."

THREE

Ryker and Littel stood under the marquee in front of the St. Mark Theatre on Fourteenth Street. A publicity photo near the ticket booth showed three pretty witches stirring a bubbling cauldron. The girls were dressed in skimpy rags that barely covered their voluptuous bodies.

"Pretty modern witches," Ryker said. "I guess even Shakespeare needs to show a little skin to draw an audience these days."

Littel looked at the picture. "Hey, this looks *good*. Better'n *42nd Street*. Cheaper, too."

"You got a lot of class, Littel," Ryker said. "But it's all third."

The two cops walked into the small outer lobby. A guard approached and Littel held up his shield. The guard pointed toward the stage and walked off. The men passed into the orchestra section and stood in the aisle. The theater was dark except for the stage. The curtain was up and the scenery for the first act was set. A black cauldron on a tripod sat in the middle of the stage against a weird backdrop of forest and fog.

Sitting around on folding chairs were actors and actresses in various stages of dress. Three detectives sat with them. Some of the players were rehearsing their lines. Ryker took in the scene for a minute, then began walking down the aisle. His footsteps echoed in the empty theater; Littel followed. They passed around the orchestra pit and up the side stairs of the stage. All the players in this real drama watched him silently as he approached. The three detectives stood. Ryker surveyed the group in front of him.

A pretty young girl in a dressing robe stood. "Double, double, toil and trouble," she said. "Fire burn and cauldron bubble."

Ryker didn't say anything.

She continued with a sneer. "Eye of newt, and toe of frog, wool of bat, and tongue of dog." She pointed at Ryker. "You look like trouble, man."

Ryker liked actors about as much as he liked doctors. Their egos were bigger than doctors', if that were possible.

"Shut up," he said.

The girl moved toward Ryker. Her face was red and her fists were clenched. No one talked to *her* like that.

Ryker gave her a soft push and she sprawled back in her chair.

"And if you all don't want to spend the night at the station house, I suggest you get off your high fucking horses and start cooperating."

A small man with glasses rose. "I, uh, assume you're in charge here now. I'm Thornton Quigly, the director. . . ."

"So?"

"Well, I assure you, Mr. . . . uh. . . ."

"Sergeant Ryker."

"Yes—I assure you we have been cooperating with your men here to the fullest. Tami was a wonderful, warm, beautiful. . . ."

35

"Cut the horseshit. Look, this Chinese fire drill is due to go on in forty-five minutes. It's Saturday night. You and I both know I can lose you a couple of big bucks in receipts if I pull you all in. It'll probably be the first time the audience outnumbered the actors, anyway. What we'd all like is some answers. Now my friend here," he motioned to Littel, "tells me you people have been jerking us off for the last couple of hours."

Ryker paused. The three standing detectives looked embarrassed. "Now I don't give a rat's ass what you think of cops, but I just came from Tami Long's apartment. You want to hear what I saw?"

Ryker told them in detail what he had seen. One of the girls got up and walked quickly off the stage.

Ryker finished and said, "So as far as I'm concerned, you're all potential suspects. You were the last people to see her alive." He turned to his detectives. "What did you manage to get?"

John Procino, a third-grade detective, answered. "Not much so far. We were just really getting started. . . ."

"You should have been out of here an hour ago." That was the problem with detectives today, Ryker thought. Used to be if a man showed some initiative, some feel for investigation, and maybe lucked out on a big case, he got promoted to second- or first-grade detective. Not anymore. About half the third-class detectives quit the force to go into higher-paying jobs with banks, financial institutions—even the CIA. It was demoralizing and not good for business, Ryker thought.

"What you got?" Ryker asked.

The chastised detective read from his notebook, "According to her friends and fellow actors, there were no known enemies. No stage-door punks hanging around. No jealous ex-lovers. No drugs. No weird religious affiliations. Just a girl from a small town in the Midwest. Real name Jane Schermerhorn. Been in New York less than a year." Procino described the parting scene at the stage door where everyone had seen Tami Long for the last time. He finished and looked at Ryker.

Ryker looked around at the actors. "Which one of you, male or female, was her lover?"

After a long minute, a tall, thin, effeminate-looking actor stood. "I was."

"What's your name?"

"Martin Seedman."

"Okay, Martin Seedman, how come you didn't walk her home?"

"As I told these other officers, I offered to, but she . . ."

"Who followed her?"

"How do I know?"

"Who followed her?"

"Nobody!" The young actor was losing his professional control.

Ryker was as accomplished an actor as any of them when he was on the job. He found it easy to pretend to know something he didn't.

"You wanted to walk her home and sleep with her. She said no. Okay, you walked off. She walked off. So how come you didn't turn around and look back at her? How many other people were on the street then? Who was walking in her direction? How about it?"

Martin Seedman slumped back into his chair. "I didn't think anything of it at the time."

"Go on."

The small stage was absolutely still. Ryker had gambled and won.

"This guy. I passed him. At first I thought it was one of us."

"One of who?"

"An actor. An actor who hadn't changed for some reason."

"Why?"

"He was wearing a cassock and cowl."

"A what?"

"A monk's robe—and hood."

"Go on."

"I passed him and looked up. He wasn't one of us. I guess he was a real monk. Halfway down the block . . ."

He paused and put his head in his hands. Ryker knew that he must be thinking about Tami's death. The other half dozen actors and actresses looked at their companion.

"You looked back."

"Yes—I looked back. He was walking in the same direction as Tami. I didn't think anything of it. I still don't think . . ."

"Let me decide that. You maybe feel a little guilty after the fact. Okay, so you were tired. You thought about following. You thought you might feel foolish if you made the trek all the way to her apartment and this monk guy was just heading to St. Luke's or Sacred Heart, right?" Ryker pulled up a chair and sat facing the man. "You called her when you got home. What time was that?"

"About one o'clock." The actor looked down, not wanting to meet the eyes of Ryker or the others.

"Then you went to sleep or did you call again?"

"I went to sleep. It was a long day."

Ryker figured he was lying. He may have called several times.

"You figured she was in somebody else's bed?"

"Yes—maybe. It's none of my business where she sleeps or who she sleeps—slept—with."

He was trying to sound sophisticated now in front of his audience.

He continued quietly. "Also, she took heavy doses of sleeping pills as soon as she got home. She couldn't sleep otherwise. I just figured . . ." His voice trailed off.

Ryker stood and turned to Littel.

"Call the victim's apartment. Give them this monk business. Question everyone again, the whole neighborhood. A monk would be pretty hard to miss. Tell our people to jog some memories a bit." He looked at Detective Procino, who was busy inspecting his shoes. "Get a full description of this monk character from Mr. Seedman here."

"Yes, sir."

Ryker turned to Seedman. "I want you to make a formal statement at the precinct. Are you going on tonight? Do you want to do it in the morning?"

The actor stood and looked around. "I'm going on," he said, trying to sound like it was a big deal.

This guy is a lousy actor, Ryker thought. "Okay, Mr. Seedman, eight o'clock tomorrow morning. Eighth Precinct. Ask for Sergeant Ryker."

Ryker turned and walked off the stage. He motioned to the three detectives to follow. Next to the orchestra pit, he turned and faced them. Littel was standing behind him trying to hide a smile. Ryker spoke.

"If ever you let a bunch of yoyos like this jerk you off again, I'll see that you're all transferred to latrine duty in the police academy." Ryker looked each of them in the eyes. "In the performance of your duties, you'll come across doctors, lawyers, very rich people, politicians, and other ball-busters. You'll come across a lot of good-looking ass, too. They'll all try to do the same thing to you—make you less of a cop. They'll threaten, they'll try to make you feel small, they'll offer you money. The women will push their twats under your noses. They're doing it for one reason.

Because you have the power when you're in the legitimate performance of your job. They know it. You'd better learn it." He looked at the stage. "Two, three hours here fucking around with a bunch of Shakespeare-quoting assholes. Flirting with a bunch of whores who couldn't care less if you were dead or alive. Taking shit from a bunch of ball-less boys. Get tough, Procino. Get tough fast."

Ryker spun on his heel and walked up the long aisle. Littel followed.

Seedman watched him go. He hesitated, then called after him. "Sergeant—tonight's Saturday. After the play we have a cast meeting. Could we make it a different time tomorrow morning?"

Ryker kept walking. "Sure—seven-thirty A.M.—on the dot."

Tami Long spent Saturday night in a cold refrigerated drawer at the medical examiner's office. In the morning a young assistant M.E. walked in and read his duty sheet. He asked for number twenty-four. Number twenty-four was wheeled into a large room containing a row of dissecting tables. Some of the tables were occupied by corpses in various stages of dissection. The young M.E. looked around as though he were deciding which table would be most comfortable for this delicate corpse, and finally chose one. The attendants lifted her and gently laid her down on the slab. The stake made a squeaking sound as it rubbed against the slate tabletop.

Two medical photographers appeared with their equipment and began photographing in color. In her four-year acting career, Tami Long had never posed in the nude for publicity pictures. Now she was posing nude for the second time in less than twenty-four hours. The attendants turned her over. The flashbulbs popped. They laid her on her side; they spread her stiff legs. The photographer snapped away, duplicating the work of the police photographers. Who took the better pictures? The police always claimed first prize. Their pictures were taken at the scene. They were more natural. Candid. The medical photographers posed all their shots on a cold slab. No contest. But when the cutting started, the medical photographers far outdistanced their police competitors.

The photographers took a few more pictures. They seemed disappointed. They had been told that this was a ritual murder, but they'd expected something more bizarre. Grudgingly, however, they admitted that neither of them had ever seen a stake through the heart.

They stepped back as the doctor began his part of the ritual. Two forensic technicians had appeared: they wanted to look at the body again. Had they missed something the night before? They wanted to look through the girl's soft tuft of pubic hair before the cutting started. Had they missed some strands of foreign pubic hair hiding in her dead forest? They wanted the tampon, they decided. Was there semen in her vagina, her anus, her mouth? Most of all they wanted the stake. Would any foreign tissue on the stake have survived the passage through the body? Yes, they would wait while the M.E. did the autopsy.

The doctor began. He dictated his procedure into a Sony recorder. Later, a secretary would transcribe his findings.

"The body is of a well-developed, well-nourished, Caucasian female. Her age is given as twenty-two. Complexion before death was apparently very light. Hair is jet-black—undyed. Pubic hair is also black. Eyes blue. Nipples . . ." He went on talking about the girl in the most intimate terms. She might have blushed if she could hear; her bright, blood-suffused face looked as though it *were* blushing.

"Apparent cause of death was due to strangulation. There is a rope around her neck. I now cut the rope. . . ." The thin hemp separated under the doctor's gleaming silver scalpel. He paused a moment and gently touched the groove in her neck where the rope had been, almost as though he were going to say, "Feel better now?" His finger left a dimple in her dead, yielding flesh.

"A wooden stake has been driven cleanly through the sternum and into the peritoneal cavity. The stake exited on the left side of the spinal column. I now remove the stake."

The attendants moved to turn the body onto its front, but the doctor waved them off. He picked up a heavy rubber mallet and a surgical chisel. As everyone watched, fascinated, he placed the chisel head on the sternum above the tip of the almost invisible stake. He raised the hammer.

His fingers curled and jaws hardened as the hammer swung home. The sternum split with a sickening sound. The doctor twisted the chisel and opened the split further. He dropped the hammer and picked up a large allis clamp. With this instrument, he forced the flesh away from the tip of the stake and grabbed it, twisting the chisel and clamp. He forced down on the chisel and pulled up on the allis clamp. It was good that he was such a young man. His face went white with the effort. No one moved. The stake began to yield like a bad tooth or a splinter, slowly at first. Then all at once it was out. The surgeon's hand with the allis clamp and the stake flew up over his head as the stake cleared the body. The doctor stood for a second with the prize above his head as though he wanted to be congratulated.

He placed the bloody oak stake on the instrument table. The girl's head and shoulders were raised as though she were trying to sit up and look at the hole between her breasts. An attendant held her legs while the doctor forced her upper torso down onto the cold slate table.

The doctor caught his breath, then began dictating again. "The stake is removed. I now remove the tampon. . . ." The young doctor gently placed his fingers between the girl's slightly parted legs. He pinched the white cotton cord and pulled. It broke. He thrust his gloved fingers into the vagina and grasped the tampon. It slid out smoothly, cold and clammy.

A strange way to spend a Sunday morning, one of the technicians thought.

The autopsy then proceeded in the usual manner.

No rape. No sex of any kind. No stray pubic hairs. A few strands of long, black, coarse fibers that resembled wool, found in the hair on her head and overlooked yesterday.

The fibers, the tampon, and the stake were all dropped into neat plastic envelopes.

The doctor looked at his watch. Twelve noon. Lunch time.

FOUR

Ryker had finished with Martin Seedman by nine A.M.
He stared out of the second-floor window of the old
station house as he collected his thoughts. The
Sunday-morning streets weren't stirring yet. The large
squad room was almost deserted. Ryker had that
Sunday feeling of time suspended until the real world
burst forth again on Monday morning. At least the
M.E.'s office was open for business. He and his new
partner, Peter Christie, were waiting for the report.

Christie was young, and like a lot of men in the
squad room these days, he wasn't a real detective yet.
He was still what was called a "silver shield," in effect,
a patrolman without a uniform, assigned to Detective
Division. The gold detective's shield would come
later—if at all, given the virtual freeze on promo-
tions. Christie was tall and very good-looking.

Ryker walked over to his partner's desk and sat on
it. Christie spoke first. "What did you think of seedy
Martin or Martin seedy—whatever he calls himself?"

"A real nothing," Ryker said. "But the lead
sounded solid enough."

Christie was a little afraid of Ryker. This man could make him or break him at this point in his career. He tried to sound as tough and professional as his partner, but with his sandy hair and clean, ruddy face, he couldn't bring it off. He looked young and innocent; in reality, he was just young.

Christie had heard all about Ryker and the sniper and that didn't make him feel any easier. He had also heard about Ryker's last partner, a young guy like himself, who had been blown away while tagging along with his sergeant.

"What do you think about this monk?" Ryker asked.

"Maybe it's not relevant. Maybe it was just a monk going someplace legitimate."

"Maybe. A lot of witnesses saw a big bearded monk in the theater Friday night, though. We have at least one witness who saw a robed man pass his apartment window on East Eleventh Street about twelve-thirty A.M."

"Did seedy Marty give you a good description?"

"Yeah. He'll be back tomorrow to help the artist with a composite drawing. One thing about actors—they notice faces and details more than the average guy. He had a good mental picture stuck in his head. Maybe actors look to see if they're the handsomest guy around or something. Anyway, he saw this monk, and he saw him good."

"Mug shots?" Christie asked.

"Tomorrow. But I don't think that will do any good. Old Martin will be here at seven A.M. He almost shit when I told him seven. He's probably blind at that hour. The next time we need him for anything we'll make it six-thirty."

"I know he's a dipshit," Christie said. "But why are you leaning on him?"

"Why not? He didn't do a fucking thing right since

Friday night." Ryker shifted to a chair and put his feet up on Christie's desk.

"You know," he said, lighting a cigar, "I'm from a different generation, maybe, but if I were Martin Seedman, I'd wonder where my balls were."

"Meaning?"

"Well, if I had a piece of ass like Tami Long, I sure as shit wouldn't wait for her to let me walk her home and fuck her."

"What *would* you do?" Christie asked.

"What would I do? If I'd had a hard-on Friday night, I would have grabbed her by the scruff of her neck and dragged her back to my place."

Christie laughed. "Girls—women—have rights these days, too. Don't you know that?"

"That's what they tell me," Ryker said. "Every chance they get."

"Which isn't often, is it, Ryker?"

The voice belonged to Deputy Inspector Connolly, who strode up behind them. Connolly was smaller than average size, about five-nine, slim, and handsome. He had distinguished gray hair and always wore dark, crisply pressed suits. Christie thought he looked like the Texas billionaire, H. Ross Perot.

"Morning, Inspector," Ryker said, not taking his feet down from Christie's desk. Christie jumped to his feet.

"I want to see you in the conference room in five minutes," Connolly said to Ryker.

"Right," Ryker said.

When he had gone, Ryker pulled his legs off the desk and sat up.

"The boss?" Christie asked.

"Yep."

"What kind of guy is he?"

"Insane."

"Insane?"

"One of the requirements for the brass."

"I don't want any crapola from you, Ryker," Deputy Inspector Connolly said five minutes later in the conference room.

"Crapola?"

"You know what I mean."

"About the asylum? Or the Zoogs?"

"Damn it, it wasn't an asylum," Connolly exploded. "I was simply taking a rest. The overwork, the stress, the pressure."

"Sure."

"And none of this . . . Zoog business, either."

Years ago they had had a joke about the Zoogs— little green men from outer space. If a case was completely unsolvable, they'd say the Zoogs did it, and laugh. Then one day, the P.C. asked for a progress report on a series of perplexing murders and Connolly had sent him a fifty-page memo on how the Zoogs were taking over the earth, starting with Manhattan. The P.C. didn't think it was funny; neither did Connolly. He really thought the Zoogs had arrived, so he was shipped off to a rubber-room hotel on Long Island. But with the change in administration, Connolly was, apparently, rehabilitated.

"What do you have so far?" Connolly asked, and Ryker gave him a rundown, concluding by saying, "Nothing concrete. A possible suspect. No rape, no penetration of any orifice, in my opinion. Death by strangulation, probably. The update comes in at one."

"Not much to go on," Connolly said.

"Pretty mysterious, all right," Ryker said. "We're talking almost . . . unearthly. . . ."

"I warned you, Ryker," Connolly said, his pale, closely shaved cheeks getting red.

"If you don't want to hear my theories, let's wait for the report," Ryker said, getting up to leave.

Ryker spent the next few hours going over the 5's, the pale-blue Supplementary Crime Reports filed by the teams investigating the murder of Tami Long. He was looking for some fact, some piece of evidence he had missed the first time around. What he found was that none of the detectives assigned to the case could spell or type.

He was making notes when the phone rang. It was Bronkowski, the desk sergeant.

"It's *her*," he said. "You want to talk?"

"Yeah," Ryker sighed. "Why not?" He slammed the phone down in its cradle and waited for the flashing light that would announce that Eleanor was on the line.

Eleanor was his ex-wife, and although they had been divorced for five years, she called all the time, asking for advice—and giving it. Mostly giving it. He usually let her yammer on about her friends and her new life in Chicago, her advertising agency and clients, the CPM of print versus broadcast media and a whole catalogue of other things that bored him to the point of brain death. Still, he liked to hear her voice.

"Sergeant Ryker," he said, picking up the phone.

"Joe? It's Ellie. That Sergeant Bronco is the rudest man I've ever spoken to."

"Ellie, this is a police station, not an answering service."

"I know, but a little common courtesy would be in order," she said. Like most cop wives, or cop ex-wives, Ellie had no conception of what her husband went through on an average day, the violence he saw, the horror he participated in, the scum he had to deal with every hour. It wasn't Ellie's fault. When cops came home, they kept their mouths shut about the job. They didn't want their sordid world to intrude on their personal lives.

"I'll fire him," Ryker said. "And you can send me one of your secretaries. Just make sure she can use a billy club and doesn't mind getting thrown up on, cursed at, and attacked by crazed crack addicts."

"I've got the perfect person," Ellie said, laughing. "She and Ciprian Delacroix were at lunch at the Pump—you know, tacky, but *expected,* I suppose— well anyway, Ciprian said to her, 'My dear, you eat with all the panache of a starving octopus.' And she said, 'At least I've got tentacles, dear.' Well, we liked to have died. Then Billy Westerling said . . ."

Ryker let her go on, comforted by her voice, but disregarding her words. He listened for rhythm, not the content, when she spoke. He could always tell when she was upset, when she was high and when she just wanted to talk, like now. It used to irritate him when she spoke about strangers as if he was supposed to know them, but he finally decided that to Ellie, the whole world was a friend, and she wanted all her friends to know and love each other.

Ryker thought her friends were too rich, too snotty, and too effeminate—except the women, who he thought were just brainless, rich bitches. He didn't love any of them. He used to love Ellie, though, and when she had told him about her promotion to the Chicago branch of her agency, he had laughed and said, "Too bad you can't take it." Ellie had looked stunned. She had assumed he'd give up the dirty, thankless work as New York City cop and get a job in private security. It was obvious to her that no one would really *want* to be a policeman. It was equally obvious to Ryker that any other job was unthinkable. He couldn't understand why anyone with any balls at all would be anything else.

He had watched with sinking fascination as she

packed a suitcase and moved out. She had tried many
times to change his mind, but the more she pleaded,
the more intransigent he became. He realized, too
late, that although he could read her tone of voice with
unerring accuracy, he had never taken her seriously.

"You're not laughing," Ellie said at the end of her
story.

"It's not funny."

"You never had a sense of humor, did you, Joe?"

"I married you, didn't I?"

"That's not funny."

"I know."

Silence.

"Ellie? I'm sorry," Ryker said. "I'm just involved
with a case."

"You're always involved with a case." Her voice
was low and sulky. He had hurt her. He hadn't meant
to, but she'd never believe it. She always took his
insensitive remarks as personal digs. They weren't. It
was just the way he was used to talking.

"Look, Ellie, I'm sorry, but I've got to get back to
work. I'll call you later."

"Just don't joke about our marriage."

It was a joke, Ryker thought. He was outraged to be
cuckolded by an advertising agency.

"Talk to you soon, Ellie."

"Love you."

"Yeah."

The new report, based on the autopsy, came in at
one-thirty P.M. The three black fibers were definitely
wool. The tampon yielded nothing. The oak stake did.
The speculation was that it had been driven through
the body with only two or three blows of a wooden
instrument. A very powerful man did the pounding,
Ryker concluded. No prints were found on the stake,
but a black wool fiber was caught on a splinter about

halfway down its length; the spectroscope matched it to the others.

Was it the monk's robe? Ryker wondered. *Why would a monk kill a girl? Why not, if he thought he was some sort of grand inquisitor and if he thought she was a witch.* Ryker groaned. Another lunatic was loose in the streets of New York.

The weeks passed quickly. Christmas and New Year's came and went. The sixteen detectives assigned to the case were reduced to eight. There were too many murders committed in New York every week to allot sixteen detectives to one dead actress. While Deputy Inspector Connolly continued to be his titular boss, Ryker actually headed up the diminished task force. Nothing significant was uncovered after the first two days, and by the middle of January, Ryker was ready to chalk it up as a singleton psycho murder.

Ryker was beyond frustrated, he was pissed. In his heart he knew he had a suspect, but he couldn't find the bastard. He couldn't even get the rest of the department to take the robed monk business seriously.

When the composite picture and orders had gone out to all squad cars, some of the patrolmen had laughed: "Stop all bearded, robed monks? I never saw a fucking robed monk in my life except in the movies. If I ever saw one I'd damn sure stop him just for kicks." From around the churches that housed robed religious orders: "The streets are crawling with robed people around here." Or intelligent questions to puzzled commanders: "The Buddhist sects around here wear saffron robes, Chief. You mean them, too?" Or, "How about the colored African robes blacks sometimes wear? How about turbans? How about Indian saris?"

Clarification came quickly: No. We're looking for a

bearded Caucasian. Please refer to your artist's sketch. Medieval monk's robe. Black or dark brown. A hood over the head. A picture of a medieval monk's robe was distributed to those who still didn't know.

Ryker knew he was dealing with a lot of borderline morons since the department had eliminated exams for police recruits, but he wondered how some of them managed to dress themselves in the morning. *Regardless of race, creed, color, sex, or national origin, they're fucking up my case,* he thought. *How equal of them.*

The one bright spot on Ryker's horizon was the gradual lessening of heat from the brass over the sniper case. So far, he hadn't said a word and neither had the brass. It was a standoff. *Hell,* he thought, *they've probably forgotten about me.* Certainly, they'd forgotten about young Tami Long, dead only a month, a stake driven through her heart, and now simply a bureaucratic annoyance—an open file—rather than a murdered human being.

Ryker hadn't known her. He probably wouldn't have liked her if he had. But he was determined to find out who killed her. He was the only one who gave a shit.

FIVE

Zachariah had been in his cheap rented room on Third Street near Avenue D for the past five weeks. He lived on bits of moldy cheese, hard biscuits, and wine. He had an ample supply of all three. He prayed and wrote and read for those five weeks, never going outside. He emptied a chamber pot in the communal toilet at the end of the hall in the middle of the night. No one ever saw him or cared to see him. He paid his weekly bill in cash, shoving the money under the manager's door. He had thrown his mattress on the floor and slept on the hard wooden bed slats. A bottle of chloroform lay under the bed. Only an enormous white candle on the floor provided his illumination at night if he decided to read. Usually, though, he said Vespers and was asleep by sundown. He never touched the single light switch on the wall. He rose before the sun came up and said morning Matins, then he read and wrote. In short, he lived like a monk in a monk's cell.

He never saw a worldly newspaper or listened to the radio or television. He didn't know that he was the object of a police manhunt, nor would he have cared if he did know.

The day he rented his room in early December, he wore a long coat over his robe. The manager noticed nothing unusual about him and never saw him again.

If a curious person had knocked on his door, though, Zachariah would not have answered. He had nothing to say to the rest of the world, for he was God's Avenger. He belonged to none of the decadent worldly religions; he belonged to the New Order, the Order of Zachariah. He had received a message from God while working as a farm laborer in upstate New York, telling him to rid the world of devils and demons in preparation for the coming of the Lord. To make the world clean for a new race of people, he had dispatched a few of his fellow citizens of Cobleskill, New York, whom he thought to be witches or warlocks. That was only the beginning.

No one knew any of this yet. Zachariah would save this good news and relate it to the world after he had progressed further in his work.

God's Avenger now knelt and prayed. "Great God, I go out into this unholy night of the Witches' Sabbat. Protect your humble servant and bring him victory over the forces of Evil. Amen."

Zachariah rose, put on his long black overcoat, picked up his shoulder bag, and slid silently out of his room. He walked to the corner and bought a *New York* magazine from a newsdealer. It was necessary to buy this worldly trash to gather intelligence on God's enemies. It was so convenient of his enemies to publish their unholy exhibitions. The forces of evil were so much in the ascendancy at the moment that they had no fear and no shame. They conducted their evil rituals right out in the open—on a stage. That would soon change as Zachariah's avenging scythe began to cut them down like so many sheaves of wheat.

God's Avenger paused under a street lamp, opened the magazine, and scanned the back pages slowly. He saw that he had a large selection this evening. He read to himself as he picked out the productions where he would most likely find a witch or demon. *"Faust* at the Metropolitan Opera House; *Mefistofele* at the New York State Opera; another production of *Macbeth* at the New York Shakespeare Festival Public Theatre . . ."* Zachariah read on. He was very familiar with the witch and demon in art and literature. To anyone else, these plays and operas were just a dramatization of legend and folk tales. To Zachariah, they were bold meetings of witches, and Zachariah knew how to deal with witches.

The monk walked west on Houston Street, his head down, determined not to be moved by the plight of the homeless people huddled in doorways or flopped over steam grates. He didn't have time for such people. The weak, the unskilled, the mentally deficient, the lazy, the addicted would be borne away like so much chaff in the whirlwind of the Lord. No, he had to face the Lord's most powerful enemies on earth, those monstrous demons from the depths of hell, sworn to destroy all that was good. He knew they would be meeting tonight. The magazine had told him where.

Zachariah walked through the darkness for over an hour. At six P.M. he was in front of the old Shakespeare Theatre on Lafayette Street in SoHo.

He sat in the front row. The house lights dimmed and the curtain lifted. He half expected to see only two witches, having dispatched the tortured soul of the third five weeks before. Instead, there were the full complement of three. To make matters worse, not only the third, but the first two were also different from the ones at the St. Mark Theatre. *Witches are multiplying in leaps and bounds,* he thought.

Witch 1: "When shall we three meet again, in thunder, lightning, or in rain?"

Witch 2: "When the hurlyburly's done . . ."

"When the battle's lost and won," Zachariah added, a little too loudly.

The third witch peered past the footlights and gave him an evil look. The audience laughed; Zachariah could barely control his rage.

The play ended and the robed monk left before the house lights came on. He found the stage door and waited in a dark alcove in the wall.

Presently, the actors and actresses began filing out. To Zachariah's dismay, they all walked together.

As the group of thirteen walked north and west, smaller groups peeled off into subways, bars, cafés, and apartment buildings. The remaining group contained only four now, two men and two women, one of whom was the witch that had given Zachariah the evil look on stage. She was a lively, freckle-faced redhead and very pretty. The four companions walked to the busy center of Greenwich Village. On MacDougal Street they turned into the Granada Restaurant and sat at the half-empty bar.

Zachariah stood outside and waited. At midnight, Greenwich Village was alive with strollers; out-of-town and uptown tourists went in and out of restaurants and cafés; craft shops remained open late and did a good business; residents walked their dogs or just walked themselves. This was a street-oriented culture. Most people who lived here took at least one promenade around the Village every evening. It was better than TV. You never knew who or what you would run into as you made your way through the twisting, winding community. A friend, perhaps, a pusher, a sexual encounter, an open invitation to a party or a poetry reading. These strange pavements were always bustling with adventure for anyone who cared to walk them. There was danger, too, of course, as much in Greenwich Village as in the rest of the city.

Zachariah, his black robe covered by the long coat, attracted little attention as he stood outside the Granada. Suddenly, the witch passed directly in front of him. Zachariah shuddered with fear for a moment, then turned and followed her with his black eyes. She was alone. Zachariah began walking.

In ten minutes they were on Barrow Street west of Seventh Avenue. Pedestrian traffic was thinning out. The monk followed out of sight; no one paid any attention to him. He was just another bearded man in an overcoat, out for a chilly stroll.

Suddenly, two black kids crossed the street and began shouting at the young actress.

"Hey, bitch, you lookin' fuh some black action, baby?" one of them yelled.

The girl had been through this before. She knew the routine. Let them talk. Let them say what they wanted. Don't get shook. Real murderers, rapists, and muggers didn't make a lot of loud talk before they did their thing—unless they were very high. There was always that to consider, but it severely strained her liberalism whenever she had to put up with this kind of sexist bullshit.

"Hey, baby," one of the kids called, as he fell into step beside her. "What's happenin'?"

"I don't have any money," she said evenly.

"We don't want your money, honey," the second boy said, as he took up position on her other side. "We want your pusseee!"

Both boys laughed. The girl kept walking. The situation was tense but not dangerous yet. A few passers-by looked idly at the threesome. The actress knew the two kids probably wouldn't do anything unless they were high on something. She had no pocketbook for them to grab. She kept her money in her shoe. A lot of her girlfriends carried a dummy pocketbook for show; most times a man would just take that and run off. It was so degrading to be treated as an object, she thought angrily.

The actress walked past her apartment house. She knew that even if her escorts had no clear ideas now, they would get some very quickly if they pushed their way into her building. She was safer on the street. She knew how to survive on the street. Three years in New York City had taught this Buffalo, New York girl, named Wanda Gierlowski, how to do that.

"This girl don' want nuthin' to do wit you, Lawrence. She's too high-class for us poor niggers."

They both laughed again.

"Let's split, man," the other agreed. "This bitch ain't very friendly."

Suddenly both kids felt an iron grip around their necks. The smaller youth began sinking to his knees. Zachariah thrust outward and both kids went sprawling, one into the gutter, the other headlong into a row of garbage cans. They sat where they had fallen and stared silently as Zachariah took off his long coat to reveal his robes.

Zachariah spoke. "I will walk with you." His voice echoed through the empty street.

Oh, shit, the girl thought. *Out of the fucking pan and into the hands of Friar Tuck.* "Okay," she said, forcing a weak smile. In Greenwich Village a person in a monk's robe was not necessarily a monk. Those eyes, she thought, would burn through an asbestos curtain.

They walked silently for a block, back the way they had come, until the actress stopped and smiled again.

"Thank you very much, Father. I'll be all right now."

Zachariah nodded his big head and waited. The

actress hesitated a moment, then turned and walked until she reached her building four doors further down the block. She glanced over her shoulder once and smiled again. She was torn between not wanting to appear rude to the monk, if he was a monk, and her fear that he might be something else.

As she mounted her stoop, she reached into the back pocket of her jeans and pulled out her keys.

"What a fucking night," she sighed.

Zachariah moved as quickly and as quietly as a phantom. When the girl glanced toward him as she pulled out her keys, he was standing where she had left him. When she looked again a second later, he was less than ten feet from her and coming fast, his black eyes glowing like hot coals. A scream froze in her throat; her fingers went limp and lifeless. She was almost in a dead faint before the sweet cloying odor of chloroform even reached her nostrils.

Zachariah held the playbill up to the weak foyer light. "Witches: Mia Culpa, Gloria Mundy, and Wendy Willo." He scanned the names on the mailboxes. Which witch was this? There—Willo and Preston. Who was Preston?

He climbed the stairs with the unconscious actress slung across his back. On the third floor, he softly fitted the key into the lock. The door opened quietly into a darkened room.

"Wendy, is that you?" came a sleepy woman's voice from the couch. "I wish you wouldn't come in so fucking late without calling, baby. I never know whether to latch the door or leave it open and go. . . ."

The woman looked up from the couch into the coal-black eyes of God's Avenger. She felt she had never seen such mesmerizing eyes before in her life. Her last thought was a memory of a picture she once saw of the mad monk, Rasputin. The chloroform pad came down hard on her plump face. Zachariah left it there. Every shallow breath she took drew the anesthesia into her lungs. Zachariah, with his prey still slung over his shoulder, walked around the small, dark living room until he found the door to the bedroom.

The monk rubbed his huge, rough hand over the wall until he found a light switch, quickly flipping it on.

Suddenly, the room exploded into a phosphorescent nightmare of witches and demons. Zachariah let out a sharp cry and reeled back; he dropped his victim with a loud thud. The overhead blacklight fed the phantasmagoric wall posters and they grew brighter.

"Oh, Lord. Thou hast led thy servant into an unholy snare!"

Zachariah sank to his knees and covered his face. The harmless wall posters seemed to mock him as they danced and glowed in the unnatural light. He prayed rapidly, thinking he had met an unholy end in the lair of the witches. He prayed harder. The prayers seemed to be working, for no demon had made a move toward him. He looked up slowly and cautiously. The occult wall posters continued to glow. Zachariah was beginning to understand. He regarded the overhead blacklight curiously for a second. Then he reached up and shut off the wall switch. The demons faded. He rose unsteadily and cautiously turned on a small night light. A weak yellow light spread across a large double bed covered with black satin sheets. He could better make out the four walls now.

He stared at the posters: Witches, deathheads, devils, demons, and zodiac signs. On the black ceiling were phosphorescent stars and planets. A large weird rendition of Tolkien's Middle Earth done in Day-Glo paints formed a mural on half of one wall.

Taken all together, it was a frightening image when the blacklight lit up the posters. Zachariah breathed deeply. Truly there was an unholy presence in this room, but he vaguely understood that this collection of pictures couldn't harm him for the moment.

His confidence returned. He explored the room and found three black candles, and other occult paraphernalia. A crucifix hung upside down over the double bed, an inverted mockery of Christianity. Zachariah was furious. He quickly removed it and hung it right side up, but a shadow of the inverted cross remained on the wall where it had hung so long. That made the big monk tremble; he felt the hairs on the back of his neck rise.

Zachariah threw the three candles on the floor and ground them underfoot as if they had been serpents. He smashed some plaster figures of demons on the dresser and searched for more unholy objects. Finally, he lifted the almost forgotten actress off the floor and flung her like a rag doll onto the big bed.

His big hands moved swiftly and deftly as he undressed his victim. She began to groan and vomit. In a few more minutes, she was bound naked by her hands and feet to the four large bedposts. Zachariah removed a white candle from his shoulder bag, lit it and placed it on the night table. He switched off the night light and lit a small incense burner. The candlelight danced in the drops of sweat which covered Wendy's naked body. Zachariah contemplated the wall posters for a minute, then made a decision. He switched on the blacklight. The demons danced and glowed again. A shudder went through the monk; he was daring the powers of evil.

From under his robe he drew out a book, the *Thesaurus Exorcismorum,* which he opened. He laid his right hand on the head of the semiconscious girl and began to read. "I, Zachariah, servant of the Lord, God's Avenger, command you, unclean spirit, if you lie hid in the body of this woman created by God, or if you vex her in any way, that you immediately give me some manifest sign of the certainty of your presence in possessing this woman."

The actress opened her eyes abruptly. "This is some kind of a fucking nightmare," she whispered.

Zachariah stared hard at her, and began reading again by the light of the candle. He recited the litany and the Fifty-fourth Psalm, then bent close over his victim.

"Devil, tell me thy name, the day and the hour thou hast entered the body of Wendy Willo."

"My real name's Wanda Gierlowski," she said. "Wendy Willo entered my body about three years ago. Now untie these fucking ropes."

"Foul and unclean spirit!" Zachariah shouted. He straightened up and began reading from Luke, "In my name shall thou cast out devils. . . ."

Wendy closed her eyes and tried to clear her head. She wondered what had happened to her roommate, Julie Preston, but dared not ask. Maybe she was out somewhere or maybe she already had the devil exorcised from her and was having coffee in the living room.

Wendy Willo knew that she was being exorcised. She recognized the hated ritual because she really *was* a witch.

The monk finished the Gospel and placed his hand on Wendy's head again. She remained motionless, while he continued the rite of exorcism.

"I exorcise thee, most vile spirit, enemy of our race, to get thee out and flee from this creature of God. . . ."

Wendy Willo belonged to one of the fun-type sexually oriented witch covens that dotted Greenwich Village. She only half believed, but the sexual orgies following the Black Mass were real enough. That's where she had met her roommate. They had become lovers and moved in together. Now, she was being exorcised by some mad monk. *Jesus.*

If she kept her head, she thought, she might get out of this all right.

"Hear, therefore, and fear, O Satan, producer of death, thief of life, seducer, betrayer of nations. . . ."

She knew about the killing on East Eleventh Street before Christmas and she, like all practicing witches, knew that the date of the killing, December 21, was the witches' midwinter Sabbat, the Festival of Yule. Tonight, February 2, was the Sabbat of Brigid and she wished now that she and Julie had gone to the meeting. Instead, they'd decided to stay home, because Julie was becoming jealous. She didn't want to share Wendy with other women as their lesbian attachment grew more intense. They were also becoming revolted at the idea of having to couple with men at these Grand Sabbats. Neither of them was a very good witch, they'd both laughingly conceded.

"I adjure thee, thou serpent of old, by the Judge of the quick and the dead, by Him who has power to send thee to Hell, that thou depart quickly from this servant of God, Wendy Willo. . . ."

The monk's voice was becoming more intense. He bent over the prostrate actress and made the sign of the cross on her forehead and breasts. She recoiled at Zachariah's touch. The monk took her squirming as another sign of her possession and she knew it. She was immediately sorry. She knew that she had to play the game if she wanted to live. She had absolutely no choice. Here she was, spread-eagled naked on the bed and no help in sight. With any luck at all, though, she could be "exorcised" and freed. She wondered again what had become of Julie. The occult junk strewn around the room was pretty damning evidence and she knew it. She tried to look peaceful, even angelic.

"Go out, therefore, thou seducer, enemy of innocence . . ."

The exorcism went on. Wendy's freckled body was slick with sweat. *With any luck at all,* she kept repeating to herself. *If only he plays the game straight.*

Zachariah began the third and final exorcism. Wendy Willo recognized it and knew that the end was near, one way or the other.

"Now, therefore, depart. Depart, thou seducer. Thy abode is the wilderness, thy habitation is the serpent. Thou shall not delay. For behold, the Lord God approaches quickly!"

The girl shivered at the deep, penetrating voice of the mad monk. She tried with all her being to look innocent. The end was coming.

"He expels thee!

"He excludes thee!

"He who shall come to judge the quick and the dead and the world by fire. Amen."

The heavy book closed. The room was silent. Zachariah peered hard at the witch. Wendy Willo held her breath. A beatific smile broke slowly across her freckled face. This was it. If ever she acted her heart out at an audition, this was the time. Her mind raced wildly for something appropriate to say. There were no cue cards and no prompters here. She suddenly remembered the Credo from her Catholic childhood. She began in a whisper.

"I believe in God the Almighty . . ."

She could feel Zachariah's eyes burning through her naked body, boring into her wide-open eyes. He was looking for a sign. A signal. Something that would tell him that his rite of exorcism had been successful.

She tried modesty. "Father, please cover me. How did I become naked?"

She tried remorse. The Act of Contrition. "Bless me, Father, for I have sinned . . ."

She tried pity. "Lord, take pity on Thy servant, Wendy Willo. . . ."

More piety. "Our Father, who art in Heaven, hallowed be Thy name . . ."

It was all coming back to her now. Her childhood flooded over her like a warm blanket, the big domed church in Buffalo, the colored Easter eggs, midnight mass at Christmas, the red flickering church candles, the smell of incense. She began to weep for herself.

Zachariah was wavering. She continued to cry. The walls glowed with painted demons. Her life hung in the balance. Zachariah was weighing the evidence. Finally, he drew a glass vial from his cassock. He held it over the sobbing actress.

"If thou be gone, Satan, this holy water will bless this child. If thou be hiding in her still, her mortal flesh will burn."

Wendy Willo began to believe that she had made it at last. Her sobs quieted as she waited for the holy water to be sprinkled on her body. The blessed water would bring proof of her innocence and her freedom; her prayers would be answered after all. Her full, freckled breasts rose and fell as she waited.

Zachariah inverted the pinched-neck bottle and passed it over the length of the naked body. The glistening drops of clear liquid fell over the freckled flesh. They made an abnormally loud splattering sound as they hit. The drops began fizzing. The tormented girl screamed out as the acid ate into her soft flesh. Her last thought on earth was that she had been most cruelly tricked. She never had a chance at all.

Zachariah's black serpentine dagger punctured her

round breast like a spatula through a Jell-O mold. The tip of the blade found her heart and stopped it like a screwdriver entering a clockwork. Blood from her beating heart squirted back into his face and over the bedsheets, then stopped. He pulled and twisted the crooked dagger until it was free, then proceeded to carve a cross in her soft flesh. He drove an oak stake home with two crashing blows of his mallet.

Zachariah looked at the dead witch's contorted and anguished face. Her mouth gaped open and her big eyes stared. *The devil should have left her mortal body after death,* he thought. She should look peaceful now, but she didn't, and that disturbed him. Gently, with his huge rough hand, he pushed and prodded the yielding flesh of her face. He closed her eyelids and mouth, then pushed up the corners of her white lips. *There, much better.* Zachariah said the Prayer for the Dead, gathered his instruments and walked back into the living room.

Julia Preston lay motionless on the couch with the chloroform pad still over her face. He stripped the plump woman and laid her on the floor. Her soft, round body was warm to the touch. He knelt down beside her and crossed her white hands across her breasts and prayed for a minute, then made the sign of the cross. Carefully, he nudged the point of an oak stake between Julia's fingers and pushed down into the breastbone. As the mallet arched high above his head, Julia opened her eyes. Zachariah was taken aback. The hammer hit the stake a glancing blow and crashed into her plump right breast, piercing the flesh and hitting the breastbone.

Julia screamed long and loud. Her arms and legs thrashed wildly, but Zachariah's powerful grip on the stake kept her pinned to the floor. He raised the hammer again. She screamed hysterically.

The door suddenly splintered. Zachariah looked up. The door heaved again. The casement was ready to give way. The monk was torn between duty and flight. He relaxed the pressure on the stake for a moment, and Julia rolled onto her stomach. Her large buttocks quivered as she covered her head with her hands.

Zachariah got to his feet. The door was hanging by its chain and one hinge now. There was shouting from the hall; it sounded like at least a dozen people. He slung his bag onto his shoulder and strode into the bedroom. He had noticed the fire escape there before. He threw the window open and mounted the iron landing just as the front door fell in. In a minute, he was gone.

The shouting neighbors who had responded to the screams now eased into the apartment slowly. Wendy Willo's screams had roused them into the halls originally and Julia Preston's heart-rending cries finally stimulated them into action. Now they proceeded slowly, men first, women right behind.

The tenants shouted nervously and took short, mincing steps as they proceeded, then they became bolder. Someone turned on a light. Julia Preston lay sobbing on the floor. Her naked body shook. The tenants were all over now. Their numbers increased as the word went up and down the staircase. A woman helped Julia onto the couch and partially covered her with the clothes that were lying on the floor.

Some of the tenants considered themselves richly rewarded for getting out of bed in the middle of the night. Others, the normal ones, were aghast at what they found in the bedroom. Normal or abnormal, however, they were all curious.

The original saviors became tour guides, pointing out the sights to the ever-arriving newcomers. Everyone poked around and touched and stared. Wendy

Willo had a large audience. She was on display for everyone to look at for as long as they wanted—or at least until the police arrived. Everyone had a turn with the blacklight switch. At least one man raided the refrigerator. Julia Preston curled up on the couch with her bare back to the sightseers and sobbed.

At last the police arrived.

SIX

The scene resembled the activity of the East Eleventh Street murder, only more so. More men from Forensic, latent fingerprints, photographers, detectives, and patrolmen. There was more equipment, more noise, more work.

Julia Preston was sedated and hustled off to Bellevue Hospital by the police medics as soon as they arrived. An assistant medical examiner was on the way.

The sightseeing tenants had disturbed the evidence. Elimination fingerprints had to be taken from everyone who admitted to being in the apartment and most of those who didn't. The familiar black powder began to spread over the apartment. Working around everyone else, Crime Lab men with small hand vacuum cleaners picked up odds and ends of lint and dust. Bigger items were dropped into glassine envelopes. Flashbulbs blinded everyone. Each tenant was questioned in his own apartment by a team of detectives.

As the first rays of light broke through the window of the victim's living room, clouds of blue-gray cigarette smoke passed through the sunbeams. Coffee and rolls came. The crime-scene ritual plodded on; the apartment began to smell. A patrolman fell asleep on the toilet bowl; a detective began snoring in the middle of questioning a tenant.

Eight o'clock. People who had jobs wanted to get to work; those who didn't work wanted to get to sleep. The cops got tired of knocking on doors. They ordered all doors kept open. The building looked like an urban commune. Tenants caught cat naps on couches and chairs until a detective remembered something that he forgot to ask and roused them. Tired patrolmen sat on the steps; tired newsmen stood in the dim hallway and craned their necks when the door to the murder scene opened. Craig Rogers, New York's nosiest local newsman, brought a mobile transmitting unit with him. He broadcast the comings and goings live on the morning news show. He asked passing cops tough questions. He got uncomplicated answers like "Beat it" and "Buzz off, Craig." Nobody liked Rogers. He'd caused a lot of trouble in the past and would cause more in the future.

Joe Ryker settled into a dusty armchair, rubbed the stubble on his face and stared at the cracks in the plaster. He looked around the Salvation-Army furnished apartment. A large poster picture of two naked women kissing hung on the opposite wall. Other posters reflected current causes and themes: Nicaragua, nukes, and ERA. A picture of the president, superimposed on a dartboard, reflected another theme—hate.

Ryker yawned. It was the '60s all over again, or maybe the '60s had never really died, just gone underground, hibernating, waiting to rise again. The kids, twenty years later, were a bit dumber and more sheeplike, with dull, TV- and drug-blasted brains.

70

They couldn't change a tire, change their minds, or change their underwear, but they were going to change the world with slogans and posters. For Ryker, it got real old, real fast.

"Where the fuck were you?" It was his partner, Peter Christie. "Connolly was going insane."

"That doesn't surprise me," Ryker said.

"Come on, you know what I mean," Christie said. "We finally get another squeal and you're not around." It had taken four hours for Midtown South to remember to call Connolly, although impaling with a wooden stake was not a particularly common MO, even in the Village. It had taken Connolly two more hours to locate Ryker, who had been sitting in his apartment, in his own Salvation Army chair, staring at the cracks in his own plaster. He didn't feel like answering the phone, so he didn't. He was afraid that it might be his ex-wife, Ellie. He hadn't felt like talking to anyone.

Ryker belched, tasting the Jack Daniel's he had been drinking half the night, then closed his eyes.

"Don't go to sleep," Christie said, the worry in his voice evident. "Connolly'll be here any minute."

"Fuck him," Ryker said, his eyes still closed, the sour mash slipping back down his throat. "You seen the corpse yet?"

"Nope, there's about eighty-seven detectives from Manhattan South crowded around the bedroom. A silver shield don't pull much weight," Christie said.

"Go find out what happened," Ryker said. "Then come back here and tell me."

Christie moved cautiously toward the bedroom, shouldering his way through the milling crowd. He didn't know any of these detectives from Manhattan South and they didn't know him. The silver shield, pinned to his lapel, stuck out amongst all the gold ones. Ryker wanted him to get himself briefed. That was a laugh. These guys wouldn't give him the right time, let alone a full briefing. He wondered why he continued to work for a ball-buster like Ryker.

There was a crowd around the bed and he couldn't get a good look at the corpse. He didn't want to appear too anxious and push through the crowd. Someone might think he was a pervert. It had to look natural—cool. A silver shield had to try to look like he'd seen it all before. The other detectives were eyeing him again.

Any minute they're going to arrest me and charge me with murder, he thought.

Just then, a little man from Latent Fingerprints walked over to him. "I'll need your fingerprints."

"What?"

"Elimination prints," the man said.

"I didn't touch a fucking thing," Christie said.

"Give him your paw, sonny," growled a hardbitten first-grade detective. "Unless of course you have something to hide."

Everyone laughed. Christie had forgotten to put on the plastic gloves and shoe protectors like everyone else.

He moved over to the bureau and was fingerprinted, then tried to remove the ink with a gooey, waterless soap. He wondered if he could find a friend here to talk to him. Why did Ryker always put these obstacles in his way? Why was he constantly being tested?

Suddenly, he spun around and shouldered his way to the bed. He looked down at the pretty girl and took most of it in at a glance. He turned away.

"My God!" he said loudly.

The room quieted.

"I know her!" He looked shaken. "I dated her a dozen times."

The remaining noise died away.

The first-grade detective sat him down on the deathbed. Questions started coming at him fast.

"Wait, wait," Christie said. "Tell me what happened first—let me get my head together. What happened?"

"Well, about one-thirty A.M. we get a call from one of the tenants . . ." began one of the detectives.

Fifteen minutes later, Christie got up from the bed. "Thanks a lot, men," he said, smiling.

As he left, one of the Manhattan South detectives called to him.

"Wait a minute, sonny. You were going to tell us what *you* knew about her."

"Oh, yeah. Well, Bunny and I first dated casually . . ."

"Her name is Wanda Gierlowski, known stage name, Wendy Willo."

Christie looked back at the body. "No shit? Hmmm . . ." He looked harder. No one spoke. "Looked like Bunny Bender for a minute there. Bunny was a little chubbier, though. . . ."

"You bastard."

"Sorry."

A few of the detectives began to laugh. They knew when they'd been had.

"Looked just like her for a minute there," Christie said, as he quickly left the room,

Ryker looked up at his partner as he walked into the living room. "They should have kicked your ass around the bedroom."

"You heard?"

"Yeah." *The kid had guts,* he thought with satisfaction.

"They might kick my ass yet. Let's go out for some air."

"Right." Ryker picked himself up out of the dilapidated armchair and headed toward the door. Outside in the hallway, Craig Rogers thrust a microphone under Ryker's nose.

"Sergeant Ryker, this is a *live* broadcast," the anemic-looking newscaster said, stressing the word *live*.

"Fuck you," Ryker said softly, moving down the staircase. His partner followed. Outside, on the street, Christie lit a cigarette.

"He said *live*."

"Did he?"

"You're going to catch it from the brass."

Ryker grunted and lit a cigar. The constantly changing crowd behind the police barricades looked bored, but hopeful. The body hadn't come out yet. Ryker drank in the cold early-morning air. The men smoked in silence. Christie turned to Ryker.

"Do you think the mad monk did it?"

"Who else? The butler?"

"I mean weirdos are always copying the MO of other weirdos. Imitation is the sincerest form of flattery."

"Yeah, but usually within a week of weirdo number one. Not five weeks later."

"Is that so?"

"That's so."

"Why were there acid burns on the body?"

"Who knows?"

"Did you see all that blood?"

"You mean all over the bed, on the wall, and all over her body?"

"Yeah."

"No, I missed it."

"Why are you jerking me off?"

"Because you're asking jerk-off questions. Ask something intelligent."

"What's his motive?"

"To kill witches."

"Oh. How does he pick his victims?"

"They both played witches in *Macbeth.*"

"This one, too?"

"Right."

"Will he follow the same MO?"

"I doubt it. He'll find another source for his victims. Not *Macbeth.* Another play, I guess. No actress is going to play a witch in *Macbeth* for some time."

Christie looked puzzled. None of it made too much sense to him. As they spoke, an assistant medical examiner arrived and passed through the barricades. Ryker stepped in front of him.

"Do you know where Dr. Morlock is now?"

"It's not my turn to watch him, Officer," the young man replied snidely.

Ryker looked down at the doctor's plastic I.D. pinned to his overcoat.

"Are you the same Dr. Sauger who fucks the corpses in the morgue?"

The young man turned red. "That's not funny!"

"Neither are you. Where's Morlock? He usually makes it his business to be at these affairs, especially when the MO's are the same."

The two men stared at each other. The doctor turned his head away.

"He—he called and asked me to come today. He's not feeling well. He's at home."

"Where's home?"

"Manhattan, someplace."

Ryker stepped aside and let the doctor pass.

"What was that all about?" Christie asked. "What's the difference who pronounces her dead and signs the death certificate? Shit, the village idiot could tell you she's dead. It's the autopsy that's important."

"Dr. Morlock is our foremost witch doctor. I wanted to talk to him."

"Witch doctor?"

"You know what last night was?"

"Yeah, Wednesday. That's the day I screw this stewardess on East 54th—"

"Last night was Brigid," Ryker interrupted.

"I thought it was pronounced frigid."

"Brigid, asshole. Brigid is the Witches' Winter Festival."

"Like the department skiing trip to the Catskills, huh?"

"Not quite. The Eleventh Street murder was committed on Yule, the Midwinter Festival, December 21. Both these days are Grand Sabbats."

"I see."

"I don't think you do. Let's go find Dr. Morlock."

Ryker left word for Connolly with a patrolman and headed off to a small coffee shop around the corner. As the men drank coffee, they waded through the huge Manhattan telephone directory, and came up with an East 60's address for Dr. Morlock, just off Park Avenue.

Ryker and Christie walked back to the crime area looking for Deputy Inspector Connolly. They found him standing on the street in front of the apartment house, talking with Craig Rogers, the newscaster. Rogers took one look at Ryker headed in his direction and quickly wrapped up the interview. He had constantly bumped heads with Ryker over the years and was becoming soft in the brain after so many losing encounters.

"Having a nice time?" Ryker said to Connolly.

"Where the hell have you been? Why aren't you in charge up there? Why is Manhattan South handling all this?" Connolly sputtered.

"Why aren't you?" Ryker said. "You're supposed to be the captain of this leaky old boat."

"That's insubordination," Connolly fumed.

"So? Fire me," Ryker said. "But it would be a *crazy* thing to do, in my opinion."

Christie cringed. So did Connolly.

"Nice suit," Ryker said. "Too bad it's empty. Now if you'll excuse us, we've got some details to follow up."

No one noticed when Connolly closed his eyes and had to put his trembling hands inside his dark Chesterfield overcoat.

"Some fucking place," Christie said, as he stared at the ornate lobby of Dr. Morlock's Park Avenue apartment. "The fucking ceiling must be fifty feet high."

The doorman, dressed as a French field marshal, approached and touched his cap. "The doctor's not in, sir."

Christie said, "Which apartment is it that he's not in?"

"Thirteenth floor, sir."

"Which apartment?"

"Thirteenth floor."

"I see."

The two cops entered the antique glass and brass elevator cage. They pulled a lever instead of pushing a button; the elevator lifted slowly.

"How does an M.E. afford this?" Christie asked, impressed.

"Maybe he does abortions on Park Avenue French poodles."

The elevator stopped and Christie opened the glass door into a large square foyer. Expensive-looking furniture sat stolidly on an Oriental rug. There were only two doors leading off the foyer. Instead of numbers, each door had a small brass plate with a name on it. Ryker walked over to the door marked "Morlock" and looked at the lock. Security downstairs was so tight that most of the tenants had never bothered to change the fancy but insecure brass locks. Ryker produced a set of picks. Christie grabbed his arm and whispered.

"What's the big deal? We can talk to him tomorrow. Maybe he's really not home. Why don't we knock?"

"Grow up. The doorman was talking to him on the intercom. Anyway, I want to see this place. He'd never invite us in, and I heard a rumor about it years ago."

"No shit? What kind of rumor?"

"Watch and see." Ryker quietly tried a few different-sized picks, until the lock clicked open. The heavy door swung slowly inward with a creak, and the men walked in.

They passed down a long, dusty corridor; Christie gaped at the pictures on the walls: paintings of burning churches, hanging priests, dark moonlit landscapes, and other themes that Christie couldn't make out. The two cops went into a large, high-ceilinged room and stared. The totally bare walls were bloodred stucco; the floor was black marble and the drapes and furniture were done in black silk. The room had a peculiar smell and was cluttered with the remains of a party of some sort.

"Looks like my high-school gym decorated for Halloween," Christie whispered.

A smooth voice behind them answered. "Does it now?"

Both men spun around. Dr. Morlock, wearing a black dressing gown, stared at them. Ryker wondered how the old buzzard snuck up behind them.

"Nice of you to invite us up, Doctor."

The old man motioned them to a black couch. They

sat; he remained standing. Ryker thought that Morlock looked younger, more alert and less like the frail old man Ryker remembered on Eleventh Street. The doctor carried himself differently, too. Ryker realized that he was wearing makeup, green eye shadow, and pale white lipstick. *Fucking weird,* he thought.

"Can I get you gentlemen something to drink?" the doctor said.

"No fucking way," Christie blurted out. He was nervous.

Morlock smiled. "Please don't be upset over my strange tastes in decorating. We're all quite normal here."

Ryker smiled back. He was looking at Morlock's smooth black dressing gown. "Who makes your shrouds, Doc?"

"What can I do for you gentlemen?" The doctor seemed annoyed now.

"We won't keep you long," Ryker said, lighting up a cigar. "You must have had a tough night."

"Why do you say that?"

Ryker feigned surprise. "Last night was the Festival of Brigid, wasn't it?"

The doctor recoiled slightly at hearing the rarely spoken word.

"Brigid. Yes. Yes, it was."

"Some crazy monk celebrated Brigid in his own cute way last night. He butchered another girl."

"I heard."

"I did some checking on you after the Eleventh Street murder. Seems you're the head witch in these parts."

"Is that so? Is this a witch trial, then?" The man was very cool.

"Quite the contrary, as they say. We need your help."

"There's no way I can get involved, Sergeant. My, uh, hobby would be misunderstood by a lot of my associates. Also, I don't think the city would understand at all—my working in the morgue, you understand?"

"Okay, we'll keep it quiet, then. We just need an expert to help us dope out this guy's MO. I thought you might have some leads for us."

"Why don't you go to the holy church fathers, then?" he said. "They used to encourage this sort of slaughter."

"Maybe, but I think they've put it aside for a while. I'd rather work with you."

"You don't mind being in league with the Devil, Sergeant?" Morlock said.

"I've had stranger partners."

The doctor hesitated. "No . . . I'm sorry . . . I can't help you."

"Look, Doc, I'm not here to twist your nuts, but you're the man I want. Don't make me run to the newspeople and tell them what a big help the Great Witch Doctor Morlock has been all along in this case."

Morlock seemed to be wrestling hard with this threat. Christie was wondering if he was going to be turned into a toad. Suddenly, a boy no older than fifteen walked into the large room. He had a head of long blond hair and wore very little. He spotted the two men on the couch and quickly walked out again.

"Left over from last night's shindig?" Ryker said with a smile.

"My nephew," the old man said.

"Right on, Uncle. I could spot the family resemblance right away. Well?"

"All right, I'll help." Morlock looked nervous. "I'd like to see this killer done away with just as much as you would. He's a threat."

"To all law-abiding witches—I know. Well, *we* usually lock people up—not do away with them."

"That first girl, she wasn't a witch," Morlock said.

"But the one last night was, wasn't she? And you knew pretty fast that she was, didn't you? The old witch's grapevine, huh, Doc? Or did someone bring you the news on a broomstick during your Grand Sabbat last night?"

"We heard it on the radio early this morning, like everyone else. One of our, uh, members recognized the young woman's name. And if you're going to make these silly jokes . . ."

"You'll turn me into an acne pimple. Okay, Doc. Agreed." Ryker took a long drag on his cigar. He flipped the ash into an inverted skull on the coffee table. "When's the next Grand Sabbat?"

"Beltane. Also known as Walpurgis Night."

"That's pretty fucking enlightening. What day?"

"April 30. The eve of May Day."

"Any in between?"

"No, but every Friday night is a regular, uh, meeting for some groups."

"What's the next big blowout after Butane?"

"Beltane. The one after that is the Summer Solstice on June 21. Then Lugnassad or Lammas Night on August 1."

"Then the biggie on October 31, huh, Doc? Halloween?"

The doctor looked at Ryker. "We don't call it Halloween. We call it Shamain."

"That's it?"

"Yes, then the year starts for us again with Yule on December 21."

"Everybody dress up like Santa Claus then?" Christie said. He was losing some of his dread about this strange place.

"Not quite, young man," the doctor said sharply.

Ryker dropped his cigar into the skull and lit another. "Early this morning, after you heard the news, you funsters discussed the possibility of looking for this guy yourselves, right?"

Dr. Morlock hesitated.

"Right?"

"Yes. Yes, we did."

"And?"

"We decided to let the police handle it."

"Bullshit. Or maybe batshit. Okay, conduct your own hunt, but if you take one single step toward him without my approval, the Salem witch trials will look like a YMCA dance when I'm finished with your crew."

"All right," Morlock said.

"Report everything you find directly to me."

"Yes."

"Any ideas for now?"

The black-robed doctor sat in a high-backed black satin chair. The two blacks fused in the dimly lit room and it appeared for a moment as though his face and hands were suspended in space.

"My friends are very rich. They have the time and money to make inquiries much as the police do, Sergeant Ryker. However, unlike the police department, all my friends are highly educated."

"Cut the uppity shit with me. Anybody who goes in for this hocus pocus has their brains in their assholes. Get on with it."

The Grand Witch held back his mounting anger. He went on slowly. "We have decided to forgo our next Sabbat and place a pair or more of . . . friends at every play, musical, and opera that has an occult theme to it. Each group will look for . . ."

"That's pretty good," Ryker said. "I must have gotten a mental message from you people earlier this morning. That's already being done. Keep your clowns away. Anything else? Any leads through the witches' underground in the city? Do your uptown dudes have any contact with the Village bunch?"

"We don't have anything definite. Also, I'm afraid a lot of these Greenwich Village people are children. They're not very serious about this thing. They're interested in the sex mostly. However, a small delegation of my friends is going around to various members of the covens tonight. If anything comes up, I'll tell you."

"Okay. Anything else?"

"Yes."

"What?"

"Well—we're holding a—seance, I guess *you* would call it. The more adept of our people can project themselves to the astral plane. Once up there, they can inquire of departed spirits as to the whereabouts of this fiend. From the astral level everything on earth can be seen."

The two cops looked at each other. Christie did a double take. Ryker rose slowly.

"Yeah, you do that, Doc. I'd be real interested in the outcome."

"I'll keep you notified," the Grand Witch said stiffly.

Christie got up and walked over to a long buffet table.

"I don't think you would like anything there," Morlock said.

Christie looked down at the buffet. The white linen cloth was red with blood. Ripped, raw meat lay scattered about, and foul-smelling bowls of liquid lined the center of the table. Christie drew back in disgust.

"That's only the ceremonial feast," Morlock said

smoothly. "The real meal, I can assure you, was very good. We had it catered by one of the few restaurants in New York that serves wild boar, venison, wild pheasant, and bear. There's some left if you'd like . . ."

"No, thanks, Doc. I'll catch a hamburger later."

"Well," Ryker said, "thanks for everything. If you need a thirteenth to make up a coven someday, be sure to call. If I need a fifth for poker I'll call you. Keep in touch."

The men let themselves out. In the elevator going down, Christie turned to his partner.

"Why'd you take a nice guy like me to a place like that?"

"Quit bitchin'. If that Sabbat had still been going strong, you would have thanked me."

"Why? I would have wound up on that table."

"They don't use real flesh anymore. At least I don't think they do. What did it look like to you?"

"I don't know. It was bloody and red."

The elevator stopped and the cops walked through the echoing lobby.

"But the orgies are real enough," Ryker continued.

"No shit?" Christie seemed to be mulling this over. The men reached the squad car and got in.

"Head downtown, Johnny," Ryker said to the driver, then he sat back and luxuriated in the rare pleasure of a chauffeured car. You could get away with a lot of shit right after a heavy homicide. In a few days, though, Ryker would be walking again or taking cabs.

Christie was deep in thought. "All his buddies must be his age," Christie said aloud. "Think those rich old people fuck?"

"Of course they fuck. He was fucking that boy, wasn't he?"

"They go AC/DC at these things?"

84

"It's part of it. They probably hire a lot of young boys and girls for the big Sabbats, though it's not really authentic. Originally, they used a lot of animals."

"Sounds like fun. I guess I'm not in with the right crowd."

"I guess not."

"How many people are at these things?"

"Well, a coven has thirteen people. One or more covens can meet together. These rich bastards do it up big. Like I said, they hire young kids so that they can get their rocks off. Some covens are all one sex, but most are men and women. The younger ones, like in the Village, fuck among themselves. They don't have to hire outside talent. Sometimes the older, richer ones invite the younger witches to their Sabbats so they can fuck the kids."

"You sound like a member in good standing yourself. Where did you get all this shit?"

"I used to go out with a Labrador Retriever. She got fucked at a Sabbat once. Nice dog, too."

"Come on, you ever been to one?"

"When you work in the sewer like we do, you learn all kinds of shit," Ryker said. The reason he knew so much about witches, he recalled, was because he had once known a hooker named Cathy. She had been invited to a Sabbat "where they fucked the shit out of her," then tipped her $500 to keep quiet about it. Being an entrepreneur, Cathy had decided to see what this witchcraft shit was all about, and in a see-through blouse, hot pants, and a cloud of cheap perfume, she had descended on a startled New York Public Library. She devoted all her nontricking time to mastering the occult and boring Ryker with the details. He wondered where the fuck she was now that he needed her.

"Tell me more about these orgies," Christie said.

"Well, if we got to Morlock's earlier, you would have got sucked, fucked, thrown, blown, eaten, beaten, masturbated, and percolated."

"And castrated. And my balls would have been the hors d'oeuvres with toothpicks through them on the buffet table."

"They're a pretty harmless bunch, I think," Ryker said. "A little S&M, a little B&D. That sort of shit."

The driver was straining so hard to hear all this that he almost ran down a pushcart. Ryker leaned over the seat.

"We're talking about the Holy Name Society communion breakfast, John. You should really try to make the next one."

"Yes, sir."

Ryker leaned back in his seat.

Christie was thinking hard. "What's a Black Mass?" he said finally.

Ryker wondered if his young partner wanted to hear more sex stories or if he was really interested in the case. "It's a sort of upside down Christian mass. They poke fun at the church. The really anti-Christian witches do it at their Sabbats. They hang crosses upside down, use black candles instead of white, say prayers with Satan's name instead of God's. It's all done in the raw."

"Great," Christie said. "Where are we going now?"

"To knock some heads together. The good citizens of Barrow Street are not coming altogether clean, but first we're going to stop at Bellevue to see if our star witness feels like talking."

The driver turned his head. "She's bananas, Sergeant. I heard about it this morning. She was completely ga-ga."

"She'll talk to me," Ryker said.

"But only if you're upside down, Ryker," Christie said, laughing.

SEVEN

Ryker and Christie walked through the huge Bellevue medical complex. After a heated argument with the resident physician, the two cops entered Julia Preston's room. The woman was semidrugged and whiter than the gray hospital sheets. She looked at the two men as they approached her bed. No one had told her that her roommate and lover was dead but she knew anyway. Through her hysteria she had come to that realization from the actions of the tenants as they had wandered through her apartment.

Ryker pulled up a chair.

"Julia."

No answer.

Ryker asked her some warm-up questions. She stared at the ceiling. Ryker spoke softly and reassuringly. He knew that her shock was as much due to her girlfriend's death as to her own nightmare experience.

"Wendy has been very helpful," Ryker said. "We hoped you would be as helpful."

Julia looked at Ryker. So did Christie. Christie

wondered where Ryker drew the line. He decided that he didn't draw it at all.

"Wendy?" Julia whispered.

"Yes, she's given us a lot of information." Ryker looked right into the girl's cloudy eyes. She turned away. One pair of strange, burning eyes was enough for today.

"She's dead."

"She's fine. She said to say hello to you."

"You're lying," Julia said groggily. "She would never say hello. She would say 'hi, baby.'"

This kid wasn't born yesterday, Ryker decided. *She's a little drugged-out and a lot afraid, but she has all her marbles intact.* He smiled at her. "That's what I meant she said."

"Bring me back a message that only she would say and maybe I'll talk to you."

"She's sleeping. But she'll be all right." Ryker knew that Julia wanted to believe him. The lie had already brought her around a bit. She was sitting up now and looked more alert. Ryker kept talking, but it was too much of a lie to sustain for long. It wasn't his eyes or his tone that betrayed the lie; as a liar, he was one of the best. It was the vibrations that she had picked up from watching and listening to the tenants, the police and the hospital staff. She knew that her lover was dead. She began to sob.

"You're cruel. Go away." She closed her eyes.

"Would I . . . would anybody say something like that if it weren't true?"

"I don't want to think about it!" she screamed. "You see what he did to me?" She pulled open her dressing gown. One breast was almost completely black and blue where the hammer had fallen. A large pressure bandage rested in her cleavage where the stake had punctured the flesh. "Are you going to tell

me that Wendy is alive after what happened to me?"
She was shouting, on the verge of letting go.

Ryker got up quickly and went into the hall. He
collided with a nurse who had no doubt come to tell
him to get out. He grabbed her arms.

"Where's the doctor?" he growled.

"He's busy. He sent me to kick you out. Now go."

"Where is he?"

She pulled away from him and pointed to the ward
at the end of the hall. Ryker strode quickly down the
hall and pushed through the doors of the ward.

Dr. Borman, the resident, spotted him and walked
over.

"You've questioned her enough, Sergeant. Medical
necessity takes priority over police necessity. I'm
afraid you'll have to leave."

Ryker looked the young doctor over. "Who told you
that? It's the other way around. Look, Doctor, time is
very critical here. If we can get some answers from her
right now, we can make an arrest in the next half hour.
It's too complicated to explain," he lied. "There's a
maniac out there and I don't want another girl butchered tonight." Ryker knew that the next murder
probably wouldn't be until Walpurgis Night, three
months away. The only rush was his own. He had a
built-in timetable for cases and no one was going to
get in his way.

"She's in very bad shape," the doctor said slowly.
He seemed to believe the cop standing in front of him.
"She really shouldn't . . ."

"She's in good shape. She just said that she was in a
little pain, though."

"Pain?"

"Yes, and since you have to give her something for
the pain anyway, why don't you give her sodium
Pentothal as an anesthetic."

"Look." The doctor was suddenly angry. "Let me prescribe the drugs. I'm not giving that girl truth serum just so you can pump her. This isn't Nazi Germany, you know."

Sometimes Ryker wished it were. It would make his job much easier.

"Look, sodium Pentothal is as good an anesthetic as anything else—right? So if it has an added hypnotic . . ."

"Get out of here, right now, and don't come back," the doctor said in a loud voice.

"Hey, Doc," Ryker said. "There's a fucking maniac out there pounding stakes through young girls' tits."

"I said out," the doctor repeated.

"You'd like to see more girls killed. You get off on that, Doc? A little necro action, that it, Doc?"

The doctor's face, which had been flushed, paled. He clenched his fists.

"Come on, Doc," Ryker said. "You going to whip my ass? A fucking pussy like you . . . a man who kills innocent victims because he's too chickenshit to—"

"Jesus, Ryker," Christie said, stepping between the two men. "Let's get out of here."

"You on his side?" Ryker asked. "Neither of you two guys give a flying fuck."

The doctor turned his back and stomped down the hall. "I'll have your badge for this."

"Oh, not that, please not that," Ryker called after him, mockingly. "Fucking scumbag," he said to Christie.

"Come on, Ryker," Christie said. *"Please.* Let's go."

"Pussy."

An hour later, Ryker was standing in the conference room at the Eighth Precinct, reporting to Deputy Inspector Connolly.

". . . so he kicked me out of the hospital," he concluded his version of the day's events.

Connolly, looking as dapper as ever in a gray flannel three-piece suit, said, "I know. The chief resident called the P.C., the P.C. called me, and now I'm gonna ream your ass."

"Save it, Connolly," Ryker said. "I'm not in any mood for your shit. I'm going home, take a nap, and run up some overtime on this case."

"Why you . . ." Connolly started, but he thought better of it. His doctor had told him he had to remain calm at all times. Connolly closed his eyes and slowly counted to ten. When he opened his eyes, Ryker was gone. *The doctors were right.* He sighed. *It worked.*

In his East Village apartment, Ryker was searching frantically through his dresser drawer for an old address book. He tossed aside broken Zippo lighters, spare change, a package of rubbers, credit card receipts, an American flag pin some Moonie had forced on him at an airport, an ashtray stolen from a Las Vegas hotel, two departmental medals for bravery, and his torn address book. He looked under *C* for Cathy, the hooker. No listing. Under *W* for whore. No listing. Finally, he found her under *H* for hooker. The Pioneer Hotel. *Great,* he thought. *They tore the damn thing down two years ago.*

While he was wondering where he'd find her, his eye caught the name Brickman. *Of course,* he thought, snapping his fingers.

He dialed Christie at the precinct and told him to go to a bar called Rob Roy's on Bleeker Street in the Village, then he dialed a number, spoke quickly, and hung up.

He was on his way out when the phone rang.

"I'm off duty, damn it," he said.

"Sorry."

"Ellie?"

"Am I interrupting something?" she asked.

"No, I was just going to sleep."

"At this hour?"

"Any hour I can."

"Do you have someone to sleep with?" she asked. She seemed to have an insatiable curiosity about his sex life. He tried to keep her guessing, tried to make it seem that there was a parade of women passing through the apartment at all hours of the day and night. The best way to keep up the pretense was to tell the truth.

"No, there's no one here, except the rats," he said.

"I don't want to interrupt anything," Ellie said, dying to interrupt.

"Well, I'm a little busy . . . sleeping," he said.

"I thought so," she said, satisfied she had gotten the truth out of him. "Is she pretty?"

"There's no one here, Ellie," he said with little conviction.

"I know you," she said. "She's probably gorgeous. Is she prettier than me?"

"No. No one is prettier than you," he said, feeling like the magic mirror on the wall.

"Well, have a good time. I'll call later—if I can ever catch you alone," she said, hanging up.

The truth was, Ryker was always alone. When he got horny, he visited a small circle of high-priced hookers he had known for several years. They gave him freebies because he was a cop. Ryker reasoned that if you had a tax problem you went to an accountant, if you had a medical problem you went to a doctor, and if you had a horniness problem, you visited a professional lady. Hookers of the caliber he used were clean, intelligent, discreet, and very good at their jobs. It beat the hell out of cruising the bar scene and picking up some broad who had VD, AIDS, herpes, or a desire to get "serious." Ryker had been serious with only one woman in his life, and felt he had gotten stiffed. He was a fast learner; he'd never let it happen again.

Ryker put the address book back into the dresser drawer, then, on an impulse, turned over the framed photograph he kept hidden there. It was a picture of Ellie and him taken while they were on their honeymoon in Nassau. Ellie, wearing an old-fashioned bikini, looked tanned, happy, and sexy. Ryker looked about the same, except there were fewer creases on his hard face—and he was smiling like an idiot. Only Ellie and the photographer had ever seen that smile. When Ryker smiled these days, people backed away from him in terror.

Ryker smiled.

Rob Roy's was a dive, a gin mill that hadn't been updated, gentrified, reclassified, dehumidified, or even cleaned in a generation. It smelled like a bar should, of piss, suds, and sweat.

Christie was standing at the bar looking mildly nauseated. "Jesus," he said. "What kind of place is this?"

"A bar," Ryker said, ordering a bottle of Kirin beer.

The bartender, a fat man with a filthy apron, tattooed arms, and a two-day growth of beard, slapped the bottle in front of Ryker.

"Jap crap," he said. "Three bucks."

Ryker threw three singles on the bar, then placed the neck of the bottle on the bar rail. With his big fist, he slammed the cap off and drank the beer before it foamed all over him. Ryker burped, then said, "We've got to get that girl to talk to us. That's why I've called Brickman."

"Who's he?"

"She," Ryker said. "She's a junkie nurse who got kicked out of a VA hospital, which is almost impossible. You actually have to kill a patient with your bare hands or take a shit on the chief doctor's desk to get fired from a VA hospital, but Brickman did it, the scruffy old cunt."

"You talkin' about me, Ryker?"

They turned to see a woman in her late sixties, small and wiry, wearing a nurse's uniform with a tiny mushroomlike cap stuck on her lank, white hair.

"Too small to be a nurse, too ugly to be a hooker, too mean to be human, it's Brickman the wonder cunt," Ryker said.

"Fuck you," Brickman said.

"You got the stuff?"

"It'll cost ya two yards, plus two more for my professional services and another big bill for the costume rental," Brickman said.

"Two bills, total," Ryker said. "Take it or leave it."

"I'll take it."

"Somehow, I knew you would."

"Try to look intelligent," Brickman said as she, Ryker, and Christie were walking toward Julia Preston's room. Ryker felt ridiculous wearing the white lab coat over his dark brown suit, but he tried to act like a doctor: it was easy being an arrogant shit.

They went into Room 811 as if they owned the place, and while Ryker stayed in the background, Christie woke Julia Preston up.

"How are we feeling today, Julie?" Christie said. *That's the way doctors on TV talked,* he thought. But Julia stared at him in silence.

"Okay, dearie," Brickman said, pushing Christie out of the way. "Medication." Smoothly and efficiently, she found the girl's vein and rammed home the syringe containing fifty milligrams of sodium Pentothal.

When Julia was under, Brickman said, "There's no guarantee this is going to work. Laymen overrate the effectiveness of sodium Pentothal. It isn't the perfect truth serum it's made out to be."

"It works good enough," Ryker said. "I've used it before."

Brickman shrugged.

They waited for five minutes, then Brickman leaned over and spoke directly into Julia's ear.

"What's your name?"

No answer.

"What's your name?" She spoke louder.

"Julia Preston."

"How do you feel?"

"Okay."

Brickman nodded to Ryker. "You have about fifteen minutes before—"

"I know." He bent over and put his lips next to Julia Preston's ear.

"Do you remember what happened to you?"

"Yes."

"Do you remember who did this to you?"

"Yes."

"Who?"

"The monk."

Christie came over to the bed. Ryker went on. "Do you remember the monk?"

"Yes."

"Did you ever see him before last night?"

"No."

"Are you sure?"

"Yes."

"How did he get into your apartment?"

95

"A key. He had—Wendy on his back."

"He was carrying her?"

"Yes."

"What time?"

"Don't know."

"What did he do to you when he got inside?"

"Something over my face. Ether. Chloroform."

"Then you passed out?"

"Yes."

Ryker continued to question her about the events of that morning but she could add very little. Finally, he started asking the questions that he knew she might not have answered if she weren't drugged. This was the reason for the sodium Pentothal.

"Were you and Wendy lovers?"

"Yes."

"Were you witches?"

"Yes."

Brickman looked at Ryker, then at the girl. Christie was making notes.

"How long have you been witches?"

"A year or so."

"Where does your coven meet?"

"In the basement of a deserted church rectory."

"Where?"

"Charles Street. The Village."

"When?"

"Every Friday night."

"And on Grand Sabbats?"

"Yes, on Grand Sabbats."

"Why didn't you go to the Sabbat of Brigid last night?"

"Jealous."

"Of what?"

"Each other. Sex—after Black Mass."

"What's the name of the head of your coven?"

"Baphomet, the Horned One."

"Real name."

"Professor Weirman."

"Where does he live?"

"Professor—NYU."

"Did you attend the regular Friday-night meetings?"

"Yes. Most of the time. Where's Wendy?"

"Any sex there?"

"Only if you want it. No orgy."

"Orgies at the Grand Sabbats only?"

"Yes."

"Did you have a full thirteen members?"

"Yes. Sometimes more. Sometimes less. Rules flexible."

Ryker continued his questioning for several more minutes, asking more questions about her coven. Finally, Brickman became concerned about the patient. Julia was sweating and becoming restless. Brickman threw Ryker a hurry-up look and the cop pressed his lips closer to Julia's ear.

"The monk. Did the monk have a name? Did he use a name?"

No answer.

"Think. Did he use a name?"

"A name. Yes. He said a kind of prayer over me. He said 'I, Zachariah, command thy soul to rest.'"

"Zachariah?"

"Zachariah."

The girl started mumbling incoherently. Ryker rose without waiting for Brickman, motioned to Christie, and the two cops stepped out into the hall. Ryker headed for the elevator. He was deep in thought and his partner said nothing. Finally, outside in the squad car, Christie spoke.

"What kind of a name is Zachariah?"

Ryker lit a cigar. "Just some asshole handle that this nut picked up for himself." He hailed a cab and both men got in. "Barrow Street," Ryker said.

After a few minutes he turned to Christie. "What have we really got that we didn't have before?"

The young cop thought hard. "Nothing, really. Just a name. Zachariah. We're no further along than before, are we?"

"No, we're not. But we do know when this guy is going to strike next—on the Walpurgis Night Sabbat —April 30."

"Big deal. I'd like to know where."

"I wonder if we could get him to strike directly at a coven."

"Why would we want to do that?"

"How would you like to become a male witch? A warlock?"

Christie gave a start. "What?" Suddenly, he remembered all the questions Ryker had asked Julia Preston about her coven. "Oh, no, boss. Be fair. Come on." He looked panicky.

"Don't be such a goddamned pussy."

"No. Look, I got a crack at detective because I busted three stickup men—not because I was a good actor. I can't pull it off. No way."

"It's part of the job. This is a difficult kind of bravery. Besides, you might get laid."

"Forget it. I can get laid a lot easier than that. Fucking covens, witches. Grand Sabbats. Who needs it?"

"You won't be alone."

"Who'll be with me—God?"

"Better than that. Abbie Robbins. I'm sure she won't refuse the assignment."

Christie thought about Abbie Robbins. He suspected she probably wouldn't refuse. She was about twenty-five years old and looked like a model. She'd been a detective about a year, and every man in the division would have liked to get into her pants, but so far none of them had. Maybe he'd be the first. Men had done stupider things to get laid, he thought.

EIGHT

Brother Zachariah sat on the cold floor of his cold, barren room contemplating self-emasculation. All the troubles of the world, he reasoned, stemmed from sex and sexual aggression. It was obvious to him that if the Devil could tempt men and women with sex, a man who was immune to such temptation could be truly free to fight evil, to do God's work.

He stood in the darkness and slipped out of his coarse woolen robe. Standing naked in the center of the cramped room, he thought about his body. It was massive and hairy, rippling with muscle and sinew. Disgusting. He rubbed his hands across his prominent pectorals, flinching slightly as his large hands passed over his erect nipples. His hands continued down his flat stomach until they reached the center of all evil.

Zachariah closed his eyes, gathering his courage, and touched his scrotum. His testicles moved in his hand as if they had a life of their own; he could feel his penis begin to rise.

No, no, he thought. *I am assaulted by the Devil, even*

in the sanctity of my own cell. He, the Evil One, is everywhere. I must end his reign on earth.

With a low moan, he released his testicles and began searching for the black canvas duffel bag. He found it, his fingers trembling with fear and anticipation, and pulled out a sharp, scythelike knife. He could feel its icy vengeance in his fingers.

Slowly, he brought it to his groin. At its touch his testicles retreated, almost as if they knew what was coming.

Zachariah took a deep breath, but his hand seemed paralyzed. *One simple movement, one cut, and I will be immune,* he thought. The muscles on his forearm stood out; he began sweating and straining, trying to accomplish this act of devotion.

Do not do this, Zachariah.

It was a voice.

Who is there? he thought.

It is the Lord thy God.

Lord?

It is I, the one who commands you to rid my people of their infection. Put down the knife.

How do I know it is Thee? And not the Devil come to tempt me?

It was I who came to you when you were a child. It was I who saw the sins you committed, the commandments you broke, the filthy acts you performed. It is the Lord thy God. Drop the knife.

Yes, Lord. But why?

If you are immune to Satan's temptation, you cheat me. You must be whole and fully human to do my work. Did I not send Jesus to confront the Devil in the wilderness, stripped of all but His human powers? And did He not face Evil as a man and conquer sin? You must follow in His footsteps. As a man.

I hear and obey, Lord, Zachariah thought. God was truly good. Like Abraham, he, Zachariah, had been ready to sacrifice all for his God, but his hand had been stayed by the Merciful One.

Zachariah knew more strongly than ever that he was guided and protected by the All-powerful. The hunt for witches must continue.

The hunt for the witch-killer was stalled. Ryker and Christie canvassed the block, checking the notebooks of the detectives who were still questioning possible witnesses. They followed up on some of the more promising witnesses, but no one could add much. Ryker's questioning was sometimes brutal, laced with threats, designed to squeeze just a little more out of a witness than had the original interrogator. But there really wasn't much left to squeeze. No one seemed to know a damned thing.

Ryker leaned against a street pole and thought about it. He had a description. He had approximate times. He knew the motive. The MO was pretty clear. What more could a witness do for him? He knew instinctively that he wasn't going to catch this mad-man until the bastard struck again—or maybe the time after that—or maybe never. The detective work was over. Just the old-fashioned police work remained: Squad-car patrols, foot patrols, maybe a tip. Someone would have to spot the monk on the street. Not an easy job, as this maniac kept a pretty low profile between jobs. The usual procedures were useless. Ryker needed something else.

He began to pick on the witnesses to relieve his frustration. A homosexual couple, a young man and an acned-faced middle-aged man, were the objects of Ryker's anger now. The two men sat in the lavender-and-white living room of their apartment on Barrow Street, down the block from the murder scene. They held hands while Ryker began his questioning. Christie sat in an armchair taking notes.

Ryker looked around. "This place looks like the waiting room in an AIDS hospital."

The younger man seemed scared, but the older one was determined not to be intimidated. "Everyone has their own tastes, Officer. We like it."

"Yeah," Ryker said. *"It's growing on me, too."*

It was past seven P.M. now and the two cops hadn't eaten since early that morning. It had been a long, long day, and they were both edgy and hungry.

Ryker began his questioning mechanically, but the only information that the two men seemed to have was that they had heard and seen two black kids harassing a girl on the street. The threesome had passed directly beneath their second-story bedroom window. Later, they had heard the sound of crashing garbage pails and looked out again. They saw three people again, and in addition, a large man who looked like he was wearing a hood.

This information was not volunteered easily. As usual, only one or two good citizens had the guts to volunteer anything. Then the cops would take this new information and use it as a club to browbeat the more reluctant witnesses. The cops had to pretend they *knew* that the person they were questioning saw or heard the same thing. The story builds. They go back and requestion people. They throw around newly gathered material. They use words like "obstructing justice" or "perjury," and finally, "down to the station house." Suddenly people begin remembering.

Ryker went through it again. The effeminate young man looked scared to death of Ryker, but kept eyeing him in a peculiar way.

"How long you two lovebirds been together?" Ryker asked.

"Two years in March," the older man said.

"Any kids?"

No answer.

Ryker stood. "Well, that's about it for you two. We'll be coming back from time to time."

The older man looked relieved. "Anytime, gentlemen. I'm sorry we couldn't be of more help."

"You'll be a lot sorrier if I find out you were holding back."

"We told you everything."

"In fact, I think you *are* holding back, and I'm going to take your buddy here back to the station house."

The older man became agitated immediately. "No. You can't take him. Take me too. Take me instead. I won't let you take him alone. He doesn't . . ."

"Yo, bitch," Ryker said. "I give the orders here." He faced the young man. "Get your coat on." The kid ran toward the coat closet.

Christie was puzzled. These people didn't seem to know any more than anybody else. Why was Ryker running the kid in?

In a few minutes, the three men were out on the cold street. The squad car was long gone, so they started to walk east. No one spoke. In front of the victim's apartment house, Ryker suddenly stopped. He pulled Christie out of earshot of the shivering boy.

"Listen, we're going into this building. You go and knock on somebody's door and keep them company. I'm going into the crime-scene apartment."

"Why?"

"Why? This cutie over here wants to give me a big B.J."

"Knock it off."

"How do you get laid so much? I mean, can't you catch a glimpse across the room, a smile?" Ryker said. "An old man like me has to tell you about body language?"

"I really wasn't trying to pick up any vibrations

from him," Christie said. "Besides, what's he know, anyway?"

"Maybe nothing." He poked Christie in the chest. "Let me give you another lecture on information-gathering and informants in general."

"Okay."

"There's really only four things that can get you what you want from people—friendship, terror, money, and sex. The people you meet on the street are not your friends. Terror is okay as far as it goes, but unless you really have someone with something to hide, he won't be terrorized. Everybody knows his rights these days. As far as money, I'd like to have the fucking cash the feds throw around for information, but we don't. What's left here?"

"Yeah, but—Jesus Christ."

"Don't get jealous. I'll get anything he's got before he gets a love lock on my cock."

"It's your party."

"Okay, let's get inside before his hard-on freezes. There's two young chicks in 2-C. Give them a thrill."

The cops walked over to the kid and led him into the foyer. Ryker buzzed 2-C on the intercom.

"Who is it?" A crackly feminine voice.

"Police," Christie said.

"Again?"

"Open up."

The buzzer sounded and Ryker opened the door. He left Christie at 2-C and took the young man up to the victims' apartment. The other cops had all gone by now, but on the door was a sign: POLICE CRIME SCENE —KEEP OUT. The broken lock and hinges had been replaced by a police padlock and temporary nailed-on hinges. Ryker produced a set of keys and opened the lock. He pushed the boy into the room and eased the damaged door shut, then turned on a large floor lamp. The boy stood in the middle of the room uncertainly. Ryker took off his coat and sat on the couch.

"Do you want to make it with me?" the big cop asked.

The boy blushed. He'd hardly spoken a word so far.

"Well?"

"Yes."

"How about your boyfriend? Aren't you faithful?"

"Most times." The boy took off his coat and draped it over a chair. He sat on the edge of the old armchair across from Ryker. "He's not much of a man, though. You're a man."

The boy moved with the grace and poise of a well-trained actress. Every motion and facial expression was provocative, Ryker thought. *If this really was a woman, she would be some piece of ass.* The boy was about eighteen and very slim. He had long blond wavy hair and just a touch of makeup. He wore a pair of light jeans and a cashmere sweater.

"Do you find me attractive?" he said, lowering his eyes.

"Very much," Ryker said. "I don't like your buddy, though."

The boy grinned wider. "You're jealous," he purred. "I could see it the moment you walked into our apartment. Would you think less of me if I was unfaithful?" The boy looked serious.

Ryker had heard this line many times before in his varied love life but never from a male. He kept telling himself to think of him as a her and the right responses would come by themselves.

"No. Look," Ryker said, "you have to do what you feel, right?"

"If he was more of a man . . ." The boy's voice trailed off in a sigh.

"Don't you worry about it. You'll work it out with him." Ryker wanted to get the preliminaries over with. This kid talked as much as a woman before an illicit sex act. "Look, I don't have much time. . . ."

"Yes, of course. I'm sorry. Would you like to see me naked?"

"Can't wait, but we have some business first."

The boy looked disappointed.

"Let's get rid of this filthy police business first," Ryker said in a low voice.

The boy pouted.

Ryker touched his arm. "I can't make it when I have business on my mind."

"Okay, okay, but we told you everything we knew."

"If I don't go back to my boss with something tonight, I'm in big trouble. I thought you had something for me."

"Love first."

"Love after."

The boy considered. "Okay. The two boys."

"The black kids?"

"Yes."

"What about them?"

"Well." He took Ryker's hand in both of his. "You know I don't work; *he* won't let me. Anyway, I'm around a lot during the day."

"Yes."

"It gets lonely around the house all day."

"Right," Ryker said. *Sounds just like a fucking housewife,* he thought.

"I used to see them a lot. We used to talk on the street."

"The black kids?"

"Yes. One day I asked them in . . . and gave them something to eat."

Ryker could imagine what, but he said, "The same ones that were walking with the murdered girl?"

"It looked like them."

"And?"

"Well, that's it. I know them. Isn't that what you call a lead?"

"I guess. What are their names?"

"Lawrence and Jonathan."

"They live around here?"

"Yes, I think so. They're on the block a lot."

"Nothing else at all?"

The boy looked disappointed. "I took a chance telling you that. If *he* ever found out that I talk to boys during the day—and give them lunch . . ."

"Yeah?"

"Well, he might kick me out."

"So what?"

"He has money."

"I see. Is that it? Could you identify the boys again?"

"Yes."

"Where do they hang out?"

"Around the stores, on Sixth Avenue. They run errands for shopkeepers sometimes. They're around the basketball courts."

"On Sixth Avenue?"

"Yes. They carried some packages home for me once. I gave them a dollar each and lunch. . . ."

"Lawrence and Jonathan?"

"Yes." The boy suddenly knelt down in front of Ryker. "Let me," he whispered.

Ryker ran his hand through the kneeling boy's long blond hair. Suddenly, he yanked the thick shock of hair. The boy screamed and flipped over as the cop twisted. Ryker dragged the surprised youth across the floor by his hair. He grabbed Ryker's wrist in order to take the tension off his scalp. The big cop dragged him on his heels until he reached the outside hallway, then let go. The blond kid fell to the floor with a thud.

Ryker went into the hall, pulled the door shut, and padlocked it. As he turned around, he saw that the boy was still lying on the floor, crying.

"You used me," he sobbed. "I feel so cheap."

"Me too."

A few peepholes opened up and down the hall. A woman's voice screeched, "What kind of a crazy apartment house is this anyway?"

Ryker wondered the same thing as he shuffled down the creaky stairs. He stopped in front of 2-C and pounded on the door.

"Who is it?" came a very attractive feminine voice.

"Vice Squad!" Ryker yelled through the door.

He smiled as he heard the commotion on the other side of the door. He could make out Christie's voice reassuring the two girls. The door opened. Christie looked comfortable sitting in an armchair with a can of beer in his hand. A bowl of potato chips and peanuts sat on the end of the table next to him.

"Why you scaring my friends like that?" the young cop asked.

"Come on, we have to go," Ryker said, grabbing Christie's beer and a handful of peanuts.

"Okay. We'll finish this later," Christie said to the girls.

Ryker drank his partner's beer as they walked out of the building.

"Did you get a blow job?" Christie asked when they were out on the street.

"All in the line of duty," Ryker answered, heading toward Sixth Avenue.

"Did you get anything else?"

"The two black kids who hassled the victim. Lawrence and Jonathan. They hang around Sixth Avenue."

"How we gonna find them?"

"We're going to kick ass and take names up and down Sixth Avenue until we come up with the right scumbag kids."

"Can't we let the uniforms do that tomorrow?"

"Tomorrow *you* may be in uniform. Maybe that'll be your first assignment."

Christie sulked at the threat while they walked through the freezing February night.

On Sixth Avenue they turned south until they came to the basketball courts. Despite the cold, a few spirited games of basketball and handball were in progress on the lighted courts. Blacks, whites, aging hippie-types and straights occupied the small area known as Father Demo Square.

Ryker and Christie walked up to a young black woman walking a dog. Ryker flashed his tin. "Two black kids about fifteen years old. Lawrence and Jonathan. You know them? Seen them around tonight?"

"Never heard of them. Never seen them."

"I hope you don't. They've killed three black women walking dogs already tonight."

The woman hurried off.

Ryker called after her, "Thank you for your help, madam."

Christie smiled. He was working for a madman.

An hour later Ryker gave up the search, forgot to say good night to Christie, and grabbed a cab to the East Side. The cab was warm and smelled of body odor, mice, and cheap perfume. *A slum on wheels,* Ryker thought, opening the window and trying to clear his mind as well as his nostrils.

The cabby deposited him in front of the crumbling tenement where he had lived for fifteen years in apartment 5-A. It was a long walk up five flights for a man pushing forty, a reminder that he had never moved to the suburbs, raised a family, had barbecues, a stationwagon, or a shaggy dog like most cops. Once he had thought that was the life he wanted, but when Eleanor had split, he went back to being an urban survivor in both mind and body.

He put his key in the frail glass-and-wood outer door, and when he turned the lock, the entire brass cylinder came out with the key. *Shit,* he thought, *fucking junkies breaking in again.* The last guy he had caught still wasn't feeling too good, but the problem with the junkie population was that as soon as you had the locals straightened out, they got busted or moved or died, and new ones moved in.

He flung the lock cylinder into the gutter and pushed through the door. The light was out in the cramped foyer, but to his right he could see the dull, metallic glow of Wolf's 1972 Panhead, a big mother Harley-Davidson. *At least Wolf didn't lose his only reason for being,* Ryker thought, trudging up the worn wooden stairs.

He hadn't gone more than halfway up to the first floor when the door to apartment 1-C opened and a six-foot-six, bearded, tattooed Wolf stepped out into the foyer and called in a high squeaky voice, "Yo, Ryker. That you?"

"Yeah," Ryker said. He didn't like bikers. They were mostly scumbag drug addicts and assholes.

"When we gonna get some po-leece protection 'round cheer?" Wolf squealed. He flexed his heavily muscled arms, making his tattoos dance. Wolf had elaborate tattoos covering his whole body and wore his graying hair in a ponytail that went halfway to his anus.

"Next week," Ryker said, continuing to climb the stairs.

"Ain't safe fer me an hawg," Wolf said, patting his bike.

"So move," Ryker said.

"Cain't. No bread." Wolf's voice was a high-pitched whistle because one of his "brothers" had taken exception to a remark and had slit his neck from ear to ear, fucking up his larynx and leaving a long, ropy scar. Wolf was no longer a Hell's Angel. He was an unaffiliated maniac, an independent asshole.

Ryker continued walking up the stairs. He didn't feel like messing with the fucking moron at the moment. He wanted a drink, a cigar, and some time to think.

Across town, at the western edge of Manhattan's tip, Christie was doing some thinking of his own.

He was in a Portuguese bar that smelled like old clams, fresh pussy, and dead meat. The place was called Luigi's, but it had been Portuguese for more than twenty years, the original Luigi having retired to a split-level home on Long Island.

Christie went there often, just to eat clams and be alone. No one bothered him at Luigi's; no one wanted anything of him. The regulars were quiet and minded their own business, content to knock back their wine and suck down lungfuls of foul-smelling cigarette smoke. It was peaceful and anonymous, exactly what Christie craved. Because for all his noisy nights in the East Side pubs, and his constant scoring with chick after chick, Christie was having a quiet breakdown. He didn't know if he wanted to be a cop anymore. The job was dirty, dangerous, and degrading. Sometimes, he thought, the women he met were like that, too. A month ago he had come to the conclusion that he hated himself, his life, his job, and, most of all, he hated the city. He wanted out. He prayed for a disability that would let him live in Portugal, Spain, Switzerland, White Fish, Montana, or anywhere away from here. He was a lousy cop and he knew it. If he had the guts, he would resign, pack his bag, and go.

Once, when he was a patrolman in Queens, he had responded to a disturbance at Kennedy Airport. After he had helped pull apart two tourist groups of Israelis and Arabs, he was washing a cut lip in the men's room. As he hunched over the wash basin, an Israeli tourist, also washing off some blood, struck up a conversation with him. He described his life on a kibbutz. He told Christie how his people had made the desert bloom; he told him about growing things and harvesting them. Christie, who had never grown anything except a few marijuana plants in the windowbox of his apartment, was intrigued. To this day, he swore he would have boarded the plane with that returning Israeli tourist group if he had had a passport with him.

That was two years ago. Today, he always carried his passport with him. One day, given the right set of circumstances, he would take a cab to the airport. It was a lot easier now that he was in plain clothes. He always had half a dozen credit cards. Someday when the city and his job got to be too much, he would board a plane and never come back. Screw the police department. Screw his creditors, his whore girl-friends, and everything else. Peter Christie would be no more.

He looked around at the silent men drinking in the silent bar. He gathered up his change, feeling very low and sorry for himself.

Ryker threw a half-empty can of beer at a mouse that had scurried across his living-room floor. The can exploded against the leg of a straight-back chair, drenching the mouse, who looked reproachfully at his attacker.

"Get back in your hole, damn it," Ryker yelled, but the mouse stood up on his hind legs and glared at him balefully.

"Fuck it," Ryker said. "Stay. Nobody gives a shit what I say, anyway."

He looked around the frayed and cluttered room, trying to remember when the furniture—and his life—was new and bright. Had it really been five years since Eleanor had left? Left him for a job. Or perhaps he had left her—for his job. As far as Ryker was concerned, he was born the day he first hit the streets in uniform; he had forgotten his childhood in Germantown in the east Eighties; he had forgotten his mother, who had died when he was eight; he had forgotten his father, who had struggled along for ten years, trying to make a home for him and pursue a career as a full-time alcoholic. Ryker had forgotten everything he wanted to forget, but no matter how hard he tried, Ellie was always on his mind.

Ryker heaved himself up from the dusty brown armchair and lumbered into the kitchen for another beer. This time he drained half the can and filled it back up to the top with bourbon. He took a slug and wandered into the bedroom.

Placing the cold can on a pile of dirty laundry, he stripped off his dark brown suit, white synthetic shirt, and striped tie. Carefully, he hung the tie, still knotted, on a hook in the closet where it joined four identical ties that were knotted and ready to wear. He kicked the brown suit into a corner and noted that he had only two more clean suits left—each one brown and each one purchased at a discount men's store. He'd have to go to the Chink laundry soon, he thought. The damned Chinaman always handled his clothes as if they were radioactive.

114

In his underwear, he went back to the living room and for no particular reason dialed Eleanor's number. When she answered, he could hear music in the background. He didn't speak. But through some sort of telepathy, she knew it was him. "Joe, how are you?" she asked. "All alone for a change?"

"All alone," he said, scratching his crotch. "As usual."

"I was just saying to Gordon and Larry that you would make a sensational model for our new campaign . . . designer briefs," Ellie said. "Billboards, print, TV, radio . . . big stuff. We're looking for a rugged model to pose for the ads."

Ryker looked down at his ragged gray boxer shorts with frayed elastic and a shredded left leg. "I'd be perfect," he said. "You should see me now." He belched and stopped scratching. "You giving a party?" he asked.

"Not really," she said. "Just the guys and girls from the office, an off-campus brainstorming session."

"About underpants?"

"Briefs, designer briefs, in a rainbow of colors. Low-cut, low-slung . . ."

"Sounds exciting," he said, taking a gulp of his drink. "Anybody out there that can fill a pair of briefs?"

"You'd be surprised," she said in her seductive voice.

"I'm sure I would," he said, catching a movement out of the corner of his eye. It was the mouse. "Look, Ellie, I got to go. I got company," he said, eyeing the small brown creature as it prowled the perimeter of the room.

"Don't you ever stop?" she said. "God, you must be exhausted with all those women."

"This one's a mousy little thing."

"I'll bet. Did you call just to hear my voice?"

"That's right."

"I do that, too," she said.

"Goodbye," he said.

"Goodbye, Joe."

Eight blocks from the murder scene, in a bar called O'Donnell's County Cork, Christie had decided to leave town.

"You ever been to Israel?" he asked the bartender, a silver-haired, red-faced man named Patrick Walsh.

"Can't say as I have," Walsh said, wiping the lint off a beer glass.

"They made the desert bloom."

"Did they now? Gardeners, are they?"

Christie sighed and ordered a shot of J.D. with a beer back. When he was done, he picked up his change and started to leave.

"By the way," he said, struggling into his coat. "Two black kids—Lawrence and Jonathan—about fifteen, do odd jobs. You seen 'em?"

"Well, as luck would have it, I have," Walsh said. "And why would the police be lookin' for 'em?"

Christie hadn't said he was a cop, but bartenders, cab drivers, hookers, and school kids could all spot a cop a mile off. Patrick Walsh might be fuzzy on his geopolitics, but he knew the fuzz when he saw it.

"Well?"

"They clean up here sometimes. Hump bottles of beer upstairs, help the cook sometimes—that sort of thing. They said they were eighteen; otherwise, I wouldn't let them work—"

"Where are they now?"

"In the kitchen, maybe. They come in through the back, and the cook puts 'em to work when he's busy."

Christie walked across the bar to the swinging kitchen doors and pushed through.

Two black youths were carrying bottles of beer up the basement stairs on the far end of the room. Christie stood watching with his hands in his pockets. A fat short-order cook looked at the intruder.

One of the boys looked up. "Hey, Cookie, where you want these motherfuckin' bottles, man?"

"Out back," the cook said. He turned to Christie. "Yeah?"

"That Lawrence and Jonathan?" He nodded toward the back door where the boys had disappeared.

"Yeah."

Christie walked through the narrow kitchen. The two black kids appeared in the doorway and slid by the cop. They gave him a mean look as they forced their way around him.

"Hey!"

The boys spun around. "Who're you, man?"

"Who're *you?"* Christie asked.

"Who wanna know?"

"The motherfucking police, assholes—who the fuck you think wanna know?"

"Okay, man, be cool," Lawrence said. He was the bigger of the two and the bravest.

"You Lawrence?"

"That's me, man."

The cook disappeared.

"And you're Jonathan?" Christie asked.

The kid nodded.

"And you're the little motherfuckers who've been hasslin' the pussy on the street?"

"Shit, no, man," Lawrence said, smiling, barely trying to hide the lie. "Not us. We got us plenty of pussy."

Christie stood with his hands in his overcoat pock-

THE HAMMER OF GOD

ets. *What would Ryker do?* he thought. Then, before he could answer, his right foot shot out and the toe of his shoe buried itself in Lawrence's groin. The boy made the strangest noise Christie had ever heard, then tumbled to the floor like a broken statue.

Before Jonathan could react, Christie grabbed him by his wiry hair, punched the boy in the shoulder and spun him around like a top. Christie drove his right knee in the small of the kid's back and pulled down on his hair. The boy arched like a bow. Strange crackling noises came from his back; Christie pushed the kid forward into the wall. The boy bounced like a dead ball and toppled backward, while the cop grabbed a meat cleaver from the counter and kneeled on Jonathan's heaving chest. Lawrence was making small sounds as he rocked on the floor behind them.

"Okay, you little bastards," the cop snarled as he raised the huge cleaver.

The boy gasped under Christie's weight. "We never hurt the pussy, man! We never hurt them. Why you gettin' so hot over that, man?"

This kid's spirit was still pretty much intact, Christie decided, bringing the flat of the cleaver down alongside the struggling boy's head. The heavy instrument bounced back as it made contact. Christie raised it and swung again. The cleaver passed the boy's ear and buried itself in the wooden floor.

"Okay, you little bastard—last night you hassled a broad on Barrow Street."

The stunned boy nodded weakly.

"Somebody came along and put you on your ass. Who was it?"

The boy's thick lips moved before he said, "A—priest—or something. A guy—big. Like Robin Hood's guy."

"Little John? Friar Tuck? A monk?"

"Yeah. Yeah."

"What did he look like, asshole?"

"Big, man. Big. Beard."

"What was he wearing, shithead?"

"A cape or something."

The boy's eyes were rolling. Christie wondered if he had hit him too hard. Lawrence had apparently passed out; he wasn't making any sounds.

"What the fuck kind of cape, shithead? A robe?"

"Yeah. Yeah. With a hood. A hood."

Christie drew the story bit by bit from the stunned boy. After he was satisfied, he asked himself, *What would Ryker do now? What would be the best break he could imagine from these witnesses?* He looked down at the kid. *If he weren't black,* Christie thought, *he'd be turning pale, red, or blue by now.* He didn't want to kill him.

"You saw him again, later that night. What time? Where?" *Why not,* he thought.

"Late. Late."

"Where? When?" Christie couldn't believe his luck.

"He was tear-assin' across Eighth Street. 'Bout three."

"That morning?"

"Yeah. 'Bout three. Get off me, man. I can't breathe. Come on, man."

"Which way was he going?"

"East, man, east."

"You followed? You and Lawrence?"

"Yeah."

"Why were you on Eighth Street so late? Waiting for him?"

"Yeah. Honkey son-of-bitch. We were gonna carve the motherfucker."

"You followed."

"Yeah."

"How far?"

"I don't know."

"Come on, shithead—before you suffocate."

"We went with him far as Avenue A and Seventh."

"You see him go into a building?"

"No, man."

"You see him walking north or south?"

"North . . . I mean south."

Christie pushed harder.

"I don't know, man. He was walkin' down-town."

"Why didn't you stick him, asshole?"

"He was a big cat, man. The more we looked, the bigger he got. We jus' split. That's it. Back off me, man. My ribs is cavin' in."

The cop got up and looked around. Not bad. Not bad at all. If the monk was going back to his lair, they had a general direction to go on. It was right in their precinct.

Jonathan rolled over and got onto his hands and knees. His racking breaths became steadier. Lawrence was still motionless. Jonathan crawled over to him. "Hey, I think you fucked him up bad, man," he wheezed.

Christie knelt down beside the sprawled figure. He was breathing steadily. Christie pulled back an eyelid. The eyes rolled only slightly upward.

"Looks okay to me," he said. Christie went out the back door into the cold night. For the first time in years he felt like a cop.

Ryker had his hand on the telephone when it rang. It jangled his nerves and made his heart leap expectantly. *Eleanor?* he thought.

"Christie?" he said, the disappointment evident in his voice.

"You were expecting Jane Fonda? Meet me at McGlade's on Avenue A, as soon as possible," Christie said, and hung up.

NINE

McGlade's was a cop bar near the station house, and that meant you'd be hard pressed to find any civilians drinking there. Cops were just too loud, too wild . . . too dangerous for the average citizen. They didn't react like ordinary people; cops got pissed off at imaginary slights, downright rude at real ones, and murderous if you pushed them too far. So aside from the occasional cop groupie, mostly female and on the make, McGlade's catered only to policemen and women with booze and a benign attitude toward outrageous behavior.

"Well, well. If it isn't Joe the sniper-killer," a detective named Gorn said as Ryker came in from the cold. "The fucking hero."

Ryker ignored him and looked around for Christie, who was sitting by himself at a table in the corner of the big room. The place was almost empty, waiting for the twelve-by-eight shift to leave and the eight-by-twelve guys to arrive.

"What's up?" Ryker asked, sitting down with his partner.

THE HAMMER OF GOD

Christie told him about the two black kids and their abortive attempt to whack out the monk.

"So? What do we have?" Ryker asked.

"Just further proof that our man hangs out somewhere on the east side, probably right in our own neighborhood," Christie said.

"Proof?"

"Well, a good guess," Christie said. His elation at finding the kids was receding; his depression returning.

"Is it worth freezing our asses off tonight?" Ryker asked. "Running all over town looking for some monk who is probably at home, warm in bed, a crucifix shoved up his ass?"

"Maybe not."

"Let's do it anyway," Ryker said. The thought of returning to his dirty apartment made a few hours on the streets look good.

As they finished their drinks, Detective Gorn came staggering over to the table, his bloated, venous face a mask of drunken hatred.

"You cocksucker," he said to Ryker. "You fucking bastard. A goddamned hero cop, aren't ya? Big fucking cowboy asshole. I'm gonna teach ya something, ya prick."

Gorn leaned down to grab Ryker, but he was too slow and drunk. Ryker dodged the detective's meaty hands, grabbed Gorn's garish purple tie, and pulled straight down. Gorn's head smashed into the marble-topped table with a ripe, melonish sound; he slid to the floor in an unconscious heap.

"What's his problem?" Christie asked, as he and Ryker stepped over Gorn's prostrate body.

"Terminal scumbag," Ryker said, resisting the impulse to kick the bastard in the head.

* * *
123

By nine A.M., the detectives who were assigned to the Mad Monk case were assembled around the long table in the conference room, Deputy Inspector Connolly's command center. Lieutenant Fischetti sat uneasily at the head of the table, while, in an orgasm of democratic fervor, Connolly gave the men a short pep talk from his left.

Fischetti looked around at the faces lining the long table. His two sergeants, Ryker and Lindly, sat at the opposite end. Three detectives filled in the spaces on either side of the table. On one side were the two men who had been hassled by the actors—Procino and Ward, plus Fernandez. On the other side sat Littel, Christie, and Wilkinson. Everyone was drinking bad coffee from the squad room's filthy coffeemaker. Some of the men ran a pool concerning the coffee. Each morning they would pick a piece of paper with words like *iodine, urine, dishwater, jizz,* or *bleach* written on it. A quick vote was taken and the man with the winning ticket collected a quarter all around. This morning Fernandez won with *iodine* again. They were running out of adjectives.

"Well," Connolly said. "Like the Indian chief, I have some good news and some bad news."

Ryker put his aching head in his hands. "If he tells that stupid joke again, I'm going to shoot him," he whispered to Lindly.

"The Indian chief said to his people, 'The bad news is that all we have to eat this winter is buffalo shit.'" Connolly's smile was wider. "His people shouted, 'What is the good news, great chief?' And the chief replied, 'There is plenty of buffalo shit for everybody!'"

His joke was greeted by silence, except for the sound of slurping coffee. Connolly cleared his throat and continued.

"Well, my news is not that bad. True, the papers are having a field day after this last murder, but there's a silver lining. Sergeant Lindly will give us a rundown." He smiled at Lindly.

The blond-haired detective rose and looked around the table. Lindly was an efficient, well-spoken man. He had a college background and felt more at home in the office than on the street. Connolly leaned on him heavily for his administrative abilities.

"All right, gentlemen," he began. "The latest development is this—yesterday we phone-canvassed theaters in New York. We got lucky right off, at Lincoln Center. A robed monk made reservations for *Faust.* Now, this is an opera about a man who sells his soul to the Devil. The reservation was made in person by this robed monk in the name of Brother John. I guess that's monk's equivalent of Joe Smith. It was made for the night of April 30, which we all know now is Walpurgis Night—right? So I went down to the theater and got a description from the ticket guy. Big, bearded, piercing eyes, and all that bullshit. Sounds like our guy—right? Okay, this monk guy had a *New York* magazine with him, by the way. Next I walked over to the New York City Opera, also in Lincoln Center. On June 21, which is the Sabbat of the summer solstice, they're doing *Mefistofele,* which is Italian for *Mephistopheles*—the Devil. Brother John snagged a ticket for that one, too."

He paused but no one asked a question.

"Right," Lindly said. "Anyway, August 1 is Lugnassad or Lammas Night, another witches' Sabbat. We're all up on this good shit—right? Okay, we can all see the connection here. Big monk—makes reservations for opera with devil and witch themes—reservations made on witches' Sabbat nights. No chance of coincidence—right?"

Lindly looked around the table. Everyone seemed pleased with the break in the case. This was it. Just a mop-up operation now.

"Okay," he continued, "but we don't rest on our laurels. We still don't have him, and when we grab him, we need a case for the D.A.—right? We got a smudged set of prints from that glass vial that he used to pour acid on poor Wendy Willo. We know he touched that. So we matched those prints around the room. We have at least nine other prints all belonging to the man who touched the vial—the perp. We ran them through BCI, but we got no make. This guy is clean. When we round up Brother John, I'm sure his prints will match the ones on the vial. We also have the wool fibers that should match the ones in his robe. I don't know if this will be good enough for a jury. *We'll* know, though. We could use some more evidence—but there's no doubt in my mind that Brother John is the murderer." Lindly looked pleased with himself.

Ryker said to Lindly, "Now all we need is Brother John."

"Fuck you," Lindly said.

"You have something to say, Sergeant?" Connolly asked Ryker.

"I'm not very impressed with lab work or 'telephone-canvassing,'" Ryker replied with a yawn.

"You're old-fashioned," Lindly said.

Ryker knew that Lindly was right. Lindly had a fine mind and was the kind of cop who tied up the loose ends for the district attorney. He was a more modern type of policeman, and Ryker's breed was dying fast. The result: fewer arrests, but a higher percentage of convictions and plea bargainings. The courts were making the cops into lawyers. The head-busters were disappearing; pounding the pavements was giving way to telephones, electronics, charts, graphs, and rules of evidence. It was good and it was bad.

"I *am* old-fashioned," Ryker admitted. "It's more fun. Christie is my student. He kicked a kid in the balls last night. He never had so much fun in his life."

Christie looked uncomfortable as everyone stared at him. Fischetti shot out of his chair.

"You did *what?*"

"Well, I . . ."

"A black kid, too," Ryker added. "Under sixteen. A juvenile."

"What!" Fischetti was near panic. "Did he attack you? He attacked you, right?"

Christie looked confused. "No. Not really . . ."

"Why did you kick him in the balls? Why?" Fischetti was a political animal. He always knew which way the wind was blowing and it wasn't blowing the right way to kick black kids in the balls this year. Maybe next year.

"Well, shit. I mean, I felt like it. He deserved it. I hit the other one with a meat cleaver, too."

"Oh, my God. Sweet swinging Jesus." Fischetti fell back in his chair, looking to Connolly for help. But the deputy inspector maintained a stony silence.

Ryker was trying not to laugh; Lindly still looked annoyed. The rest of the detectives were smiling into their coffee mugs.

"They were hassling women on the street down in the Village," said Christie sulkily. "So what?"

"So you kicked one in the balls," Fischetti sighed. "And you hit the other one with a meat cleaver. Sure. Sure. Why not?" He looked sad.

At the words *meat cleaver,* a few of the other men broke into audible laughter.

"Sure. Sure. Funny. Funny. This is why the police . . ."

Ryker stood. "Okay. Enough of this. Let's get back to Brother John, alias the Mad Monk, alias Zachariah. Christie kicked that kid in the balls for a perfectly good cause."

At the name Zachariah, everyone looked at Ryker. This was something new. Lindly sat down. He knew Ryker probably had something and that he was about to take over the meeting. He could see it in his burning eyes. He respected this tough but crude cop, despite their differences in approaching a problem. He was glad Ryker was around to do the dirty work.

"Okay," Ryker began. "Yesterday after I left the crime scene, Christie and I went to see Dr. Morlock— the assistant M.E.—at his apartment."

"Why?" Fischetti interrupted. "Did you want to kick him in the balls, too?"

"Actually, I did, but he's getting on in years, you know? A small target. Anyway, it seems—and what I'm about to say will not leave this room—it seems the good doctor is a witch. A male witch. A warlock. Morlock the warlock."

"And my grandmother is Count Dracula," Lindly mumbled.

"The good doctor put me on to a few things," Ryker continued, ignoring the interruption.

Everyone sat back as Ryker related his conversation with Dr. Morlock. The detectives were fascinated. Ryker always came back with a good story when he was out on the prowl. The room was still. Ryker concluded his story about Morlock and witchcraft in general. He paused for a reaction.

"Wait a minute," Connolly said, finally. "This makes no sense. First of all, you had no business going in there. The man's an assistant M.E."

Fischetti, always on the lookout for improprieties, was cringing.

"Hold on," Ryker said. "I don't care how this guy

gets his jollies. I don't give a rat's ass if he uses the cadavers' balls in his martinis. I told you I gave him my word he wouldn't be publicly involved. We have more important things to do here."

"So what about this Zachariah thing? How did you get that name?" Connolly asked.

Ryker knew that Morlock's job with the city was finished and maybe his medical career, too, unless he got Connolly alone and threatened to bash his head in if he opened his mouth. He didn't care for Morlock, but a promise was a promise.

"Look, just keep in mind that we may need him later as an expert witness. Don't rock the fucking boat, Inspector."

"What about Zachariah?"

"We went to Bellevue. Julia Preston told me that that's what the monk called himself as he was saying the Prayer for the Dead over her."

"She told you that? She wouldn't say anything to Wilkinson and Fernandez when they got her to the hospital in the morning," Fischetti said. "They went back later—last night. Right, men?"

Wilkinson and Fernandez nodded. Wilkinson said, "She wouldn't say shit, couldn't say shit. She was a little hysterical."

Fischetti looked at Ryker. "What did you do, offer to cut her throat?"

"You don't really want to know, do you?" Ryker said.

"I see," Fischetti said. "Sure. Okay. Are we getting sued for a hundred or two hundred million?"

The other detectives hid their faces in their coffee mugs, notebooks, and hands. Fischetti was exasperated.

"Please continue," Connolly said.

"Get to the part where Christie kicks the kids in the balls," Lindly said. "We all want to hear that."

Grins broke into laughter again. Christie turned red.

"And the meat cleaver. Don't forget the meat cleaver," Littel added.

Ryker gave them a heavily edited version of his day, omitting the Pentothal injection and his encounter with the gay kid, and ended by saying, "Christie and me were pounding leather all night, trying to get a make on this guy. A hotel desk man claims to have seen him, carrying a black canvas bag on the night of Willo's murder, but you know the neighborhood. Ain't nobody sayin' nothin' 'bout nobody."

"You had quite a busy day, Ryker," Lindly said. "Too bad it was mostly for nothing. You really should call the station house once in a while. You would have known about the make we got at Lincoln Center. You work here too, you know. We won't keep secrets from you if you call."

"Fuck you. This case has a long way to go yet."

"Does it?"

"That's right. I have a few plans we can toss around."

"Let's have them," Connolly said, looking at his watch. He had to take his tranquilizers in ten minutes.

"What I want to do is to have Christie infiltrate a witches' coven," Ryker said. "The coven Wendy Willo and Julia Preston belonged to. I suppose they have some openings now. He should go in with a female. I'm thinking of Detective Robbins. I'm thinking of joining Morlock's coven. Maybe I'll take a partner."

"Wait a minute," Lindly said. "What for? We're going to nail his unholy asshole on April 30, at Lincoln Center."

The other detectives nodded slowly and mumbled agreement. Christie was a little depressed. It seemed to him that all their work last night was for nothing. In his mind he pictured red flowers blooming in the desert and wished he were there.

Ryker looked around the table. "Are you going to wait for him to come to you? Are we going to react to him or are we going to act? Children react to situations. We're supposed to make things happen. What if he gets shy and decides to stay away from this April 30 thing at Lincoln Center? Everyone will be standing around with their fingers up their asses, watching some asshole opera, while Zach is watching some college production of something else up in the Bronx. We have to present him with an absolutely irresistible target—a whole coven of witches."

"Listen, Ryker," Fischetti piped in. "I don't want to pull him away from his original target if he's got intentions of hitting it. Sometimes a back-up scheme like this backfires. You know what I mean?"

"How many other theaters in the metropolitan area did you telephone wizards check for April 30? Probably not one after you hit gold at Lincoln Center. You think maybe he doesn't have a back-up plan, too?"

Lindly looked uncomfortable. "Okay. So we'll check them now. How many theaters could be running a production with an occult or a satanic theme on April 30?"

"It's not a matter of how many—it's a matter of where. There's no complete theater listing outside of Manhattan. There must be close to five hundred college, high school, drama club, and other amateur productions in the boroughs and suburbs. Okay, Zach picks up a stray flyer or he reads a small announcement somewhere or he sees a notice plastered on a wall. He reads that *The Night of the Cock-Eating Witches* or something will be produced by the East Bumfuck Civic Association at the Memorial Auditorium. He decides he'd rather go there instead. Maybe he knows Manhattan's hot, so he takes a subway and pops up in East Bumfuck. He pins some amateur actress to a bed with an oak toothpick while we're groaning through some dipshit opera at Lincoln Center. No good. No fucking good."

"It seems to me we could still cover every theater that he might hit on April 30," Lindly said.

"Yeah, if we don't do much else that night," Ryker said. "First, some of these productions are last-minute decisions, right? Second, there are about ten counties around the metropolitan area that can be reached by public transportation. I don't want some yokel suburban cop doing my job. I want the action on my turf right here in town. Third, if this scumbag changes his MO, he might decide that some passing hooker is a witch on the night of April 30. He may decide that the Rockettes at Radio City are a string of witches and wipe them out. This guy is loosely wrapped. He might not wait for Walpurgis Night on April 30. Every Friday night is a regular minor Sabbat. Walpurgis Night and Lammas Night and Halloween and the rest of them are just the biggies. He may just jump the gun. It's a long time between Brigid and Walpurgis. I'm not waiting for Brother John to come to me at Lincoln Center just because he bought a fucking ticket."

Christie was smiling. He had visions of himself prancing around naked at a Sabbat orgy with Detective Abigail Robbins. Everyone else was deep in his own thoughts.

Fischetti leaned back in his chair. He looked at Connolly.

"What's your plan? How can you get him to hit a coven?" Connolly asked, wishing he had the balls to pull out his tranquilizers and swallow them in front of the men.

Ryker lit a stumpy cigar. "First things first. We have a fix on his address, right?"

"That's the important thing," Lindly agreed. "I'd like to nab him before April 30, too."

Fischetti rose and walked over to a wall map of the Eighth Precinct. "Okay, what do we have here? Let's see." He stared at the big map for a full minute.

"He could be anywhere," Fischetti said at last. "Any one of these old buildings, down by the river, hiding in the basement of the Baruch houses—"

"Or living in a wrecked car, a cardboard box, or a tree in East River Park." Ryker cut in. "What's the chances of getting the manpower on this thing?"

Connolly cleared his throat. "Slim to none."

"So a house-to-house is out of the question?" Ryker asked.

"Selective coverage only," Connolly said, reaching into his suit coat pocket for the little yellow pills that made the Zoogs go away.

"Yeah, two assholes from the rubber-gun squad and us, right?" Ryker asked.

"Well, uh," Connolly began, pulling the vial of pills from his pocket.

"This is a real important case, I see," Ryker continued. "Lots of help from HQ."

"It's of the utmost—"

"Which is why you're here, right?"

"That's quite enough."

"No, it's not enough, but fuck it. We'll have to do the best we can. Maybe we can 'selectively' question as many people as possible." Ryker paused while Connolly's trembling hand pushed two pills into his dry mouth. "Uppers or downers?" Ryker asked.

Connolly glared at him.

"Come on, Inspector. Pass 'em around. We could all use a lift or a good downer."

"Shut up, Ryker," Fischetti yelled. The last thing in the world he wanted was a confrontation. It wasn't politically expedient.

"Tell us about your back-up plan," he said, hoping to quell the air of unease in the room. "We might as well give it a run in the event an all-points doesn't turn him up and in the event he doesn't show at Lincoln Center."

Ryker eyed Connolly and relit his cigar. "Okay. We assume that this guy reads some news source for his tip-offs on what's playing around town. He was seen with a *New York* magazine. We could also assume that he would pick up a copy of *Variety* or some other publication like regular newspapers that list shows. In these publications, we plant an ad—a sort of announcement, giving the time and place of a coven meeting. The *Village Voice* carries these notices for real sometimes, so it wouldn't look too out of place."

"How do we know he'll ever see it?" Lindly asked.

"We don't. But we have to try. Look, we stick the announcement in the entertainment section of each newspaper and magazine. I can't imagine that he won't buy one of these before April 30. That's his MO. If you buy tickets to something, you have the time and place on the ticket. In this case he doesn't have the tickets. He has to pick them up an hour before show time. What does he do? A week or a day before the event, he buys a paper or magazine and glances through it to see if all systems are still go. Maybe he looks to see if something better is going on that day. Okay, so old Zach picks up a *New York* magazine, or the *Daily News,* let's say. He wants to check his times. Maybe he wants to do a double-header that day. He turns to the pages with the plays and—shit—there's a box ad for a coven meeting. There's a picture of something to do with witchcraft, but nothing so obvious that everyone would notice. Something only a

witch or a witch-hunter would know. We get Morlock
for that. We put the time and place of the coven
meeting in Latin—"

"Latin? Why Latin? How do we know Zachariah
knows Latin? I don't think he's a real monk to begin
with. Real monks may know Latin, but this guy is not
necessarily a real monk," Fischetti said.

"Right, we don't know. But we can assume he
recognizes Latin when he sees it. If he has religious
books and stuff, words, phrases, and sometimes the
whole text is in Latin. He'll recognize it and get it
translated if he doesn't know it."

"What's the ad going to say?"

"Something about the Grand Sabbat for Walpurgis
Night. One address will be Morlock's place and the
other will be Willo and Preston's coven. That, by the
way, is in the basement of a deserted church rectory
on Charles Street down in the Village."

Lindly looked surprised. "No shit? A church rectory?"

"That's right. That should really raise Zachariah's
temperature a bit. That's what I'm hoping, anyway. In
addition, this Village coven meets every Friday night
fairly regularly. Morlock's group only meets on the
Grand Sabbats. We'll run the ad almost daily for the
Charles Street address. With any luck he'll be tempted
to drop in on a Friday before Walpurgis Night. Christie will be at every Friday night meeting. We'll sit on
the place each time, too."

"What else will this ad say?" Fischetti asked.

"I'll work it out with Morlock. He should know.
We'll only ask for wandering witches—witches with
no regular covens. We don't want a mob scene there.
Bring your own raw meat or something like that."

"Is Morlock being cooperative?"

"Well . . . he will be. He's going to let me join his
coven, although he doesn't know it yet. What we have

135

to do first is contact the magazines." Ryker looked around.

Everyone seemed to be thinking hard. Fischetti was wondering about possible illegalities. Lindly was looking for holes to plug. He was reluctantly for the plan now. "Do you think he'd take on a whole coven of witches?" he asked.

"I think he'll get a hard-on just thinking about it," Ryker said. "That bastard will come on like the wrath of God swinging a fiery sword."

"Suppose someone gets hurt?" a worried Fischetti said.

"So?"

"Well, I mean these people might be strange and all, but they're citizens, too. Civilians. I think maybe we should inform them that their meeting is being used as a decoy to—"

"No fucking way. Listen, it's got to appear to be just what it is—a witches' coven holding a meeting, period. If the shit hits the fan, Christie and I can handle it. I don't think this guy will have a firearm, anyway. Probably a club or a sword or some such fucking thing. We'll have the back-up teams around both locations. He is a *big* motherfucker."

"This sounds like a good excuse for you and Christie to get your rocks off at the Walpurgis Night orgy you mentioned before, Ryker," Lindly said.

"You want to take my place? If you're so sure the monk won't show, you can take my place and get laid. Tell your wife you're working late. I'll keep her company."

"Very funny." Lindly hesitated a moment. "No. No, I don't think I'll go. I'd rather be at the opera."

"Figures," Ryker said, sitting down. The detectives fell into animated conversation. The details of the operation were hammered out; Christie phoned for sandwiches; calls were made for clearances; and the main points of the plan were gone over again. The meeting was coming to a close. As usual, Ryker had had his way.

"Didn't we forget something?" Christie said. "We forgot about the female partner for me. I'll definitely need one to infiltrate that Village coven. It'll be a good cover. I'd like to take Detective Robbins."

"I'm sure you would," Fischetti said.

"Well, shit, Lieutenant, after all, I need a partner."

"Why don't you take Lindly?" Wilkinson said. "I'll bet you never seen him naked."

"Only in my wet dreams."

"Who's going to ask Robbins?" Littel asked.

"Nobody has to ask—make it an order," Ryker said.

"You can't order a female cop to pull that kind of duty," Fischetti said, worried again.

"Why not? I get fucked by the department every day," Ryker said.

The meeting was becoming disorderly again as the men hooted and made obscene comments. Fischetti finally pounded the table. Connolly looked pale and dazed. The tranquilizers were working fine.

"We'll ask for volunteers from the different squads," Fischetti said. "It's my understanding that a young lady from Narcotics did something similar once to break a crack outfit. Anyway, we still need clearance from higher up."

"As long as she's young and game," Christie said. "How about you, Joe? You going to need a partner at Morlock's?"

"Not a female, necessarily. I'll have to think about it."

"I'll go with you if you bring plenty of Vaseline," Procino said, laughing.

"Yeah," Lindly said. "Orgies have no rules. You'd better keep a cork in your asshole."

The meeting degenerated into obscenities again, causing Fischetti to pound on the table. "Can't we keep this on a higher level?" he pleaded, looking to Connolly for help. But the deputy inspector was floating on a cloud in another dimension.

Christie looked concerned. He hadn't considered the possibility of being buggered by some crazy warlock.

"Look," Ryker said, "if the monk shows, he might show during the Black Mass—before the orgy. If he doesn't show, we'll have some good stories to tell you around the campfire afterwards. Where's Robbins now?"

"Taking her RDO," Fischetti said, referring to her regular day off.

"Where does she live?"

"Check detective ten cards downstairs." The ten cards held the addresses and phone numbers of all the members of the force.

"Okay, you fish around for some other female volunteers if you want, but I have a feeling Robbins will be game. I'll check with her, and I'll also go to see Morlock for some professional advice and information."

Fischetti stood. "Well, if that's it, I'll see you all tomorrow morning at eight. By that time we'll have some of this stuff moving along."

Lindly rose also. "Aren't you going to say, 'I hope you know what you're doing, Ryker'?"

"Didn't I say that yet?"

"No."

Fischetti turned to Ryker. "I hope you know what you're doing, Ryker."

TEN

Ryker and Christie walked through the dismal February streets, looking for a cab. They finally caught an unlicensed gypsy and headed uptown.

"Let's go to my place and clean up," Christie said, telling the driver to go to East 56th Street. "We can get something to eat and some shut-eye, too."

"You say that to all your girls?"

At the modern high-rise around the corner on 56th Street, they rode up to the nineteenth floor in a swift, noiseless elevator and stepped into a carpeted hall. The young cop opened the door and ushered Ryker into a large L-shaped studio apartment. Ryker stood and looked around. The place was almost as disorganized as his own, but everything was fairly new and modern. A stray bra, like a hunter's trophy, hung from a pole lamp. "What do you pay for this dive?"

"Well, it goes for twelve hundred bucks a month," Christie said.

"What are you—on the pad?" Ryker asked. His own rent-controlled apartment, slum that it was, only cost him four hundred a month.

"Sometimes I wish I were, but in this case I'm living here rent-free while Rosanna is in Europe," Christie said.

"Rosanna?"

"Girl I know. She likes me."

"But not enough to live in the same country as you?"

"Something like that," Christie said. "Throw your coat down. I'm going to shave."

Ryker dropped his coat over an end table and sank into an inflatable rubber armchair. The chair sagged and almost swallowed his massive bulk.

"What the fuck kind of chair is this?" he yelled into the bathroom.

"Try the recliner," Christie yelled back.

Ryker leaned back in the lounger and closed his eyes. It would be easy to fall asleep in this big blue fake-velvet chair, he thought, trying to force himself to stay awake.

"I said I hate this fucking city," Christie said, standing over Ryker, holding a toothbrush in his hand.

"So what else is new?" Ryker asked, pissed because he had dozed off against his will.

"I mean it," Christie said.

"Move."

"Where?"

"Brooklyn."

"Very funny. How does Spain sound to you? Come with me."

"I bet you say that to all your girls."

Christie walked around the single room with a toothbrush in his hand. "I'm serious. Let's split. You have no family. I have no family. This place is going to kill both of us. Let's go to Israel."

"Forget it."

"No. Listen, after my parents died, my sister and I

lived alone for a while in their apartment in the
Bronx. One night, after I became a cop, a guy knocks
on our door. I was out, working the twelve by
eight—"

"I'm not interested."

"He says he's from the Eight-Seven. 'Your brother
Peter is hurt,' he says. My sister opens the door, she's
worried, scared. Two guys there. They rape her and
beat her, then they rip off the apartment. She moved
to Colorado a month later. This place is fucking
insane. Did you ever read the graffiti all over this
fucking town?"

"I wrote some of it."

"Be fucking serious, please."

Ryker stretched and sank back into the lounger.
"What are you telling me that I don't know?"

"Spain, England, Hong Kong, Tahiti—anyplace.
Why not?"

"Hey, where else can you hunt monks with a .357
Magnum except here in good old NYC?"

"You love this shit," Christie said disgustedly. "You
eat this shit up." He stamped back into the bathroom.

Ryker lit a cigar.

By five P.M., both men were reasonably clean, fed,
and rested. In addition, they'd killed half a bottle of
bourbon.

Ryker rose. "Let's go."

"Where to first?"

"Robbins' apartment. Then Morlock's."

"Okay." Christie was nervous about seeing Abigail
Robbins. He checked his hair in the hall mirror before
they left.

The two detectives walked to 55th Street; another
high-rise loomed in front of them. Most married cops
lived in the distant suburbs. The city was no place for
a wife and kids. But some single cops, male and

female, liked the throb and vitality of Manhattan. No one cared what you did or who you did it with. Possible mates of either sex thronged the pubs and singles bars, there for the picking. Prostitutes, dope, kinky sex, strange clothes, and strange parties were available. The nine-to-five straights, the bridge-and-tunnel people, about a million of them daily, boarded the buses, subways, and railroads and departed the small island of Manhattan for the hinterlands and the TV set. Some stayed, the ones who could afford it—or couldn't afford to move. Some lived here permanently, putting up with high rents, crime, pollution, and crowds for just a little bit of the good life after dark. Christie was a reluctant swinger; Abigail Robbins was a very committed one.

"How's she afford to live in this neighborhood? Your girlfriend Rosanna support her, too?" Ryker asked as they brushed aside the doorman and waited for the elevator.

"Rumor has it she's got money of her own. Family money," Christie said.

"Or she's hooking or selling dope," Ryker said, punching the button for the twenty-third floor.

"You always suspect people of doing wrong," Christie said.

"I'm always right."

They found Abigail Robbins home, which might have been unusual, except that her RDO had been taken as a sick day. She answered the door in a Japanese kimono, a tissue in front of her nose, and little else.

"Sergeant Ryker and Detective . . . ?"

"Christie."

"Right. Christie."

The men walked in. Ryker did a quick scan. *Just like Christie's,* he thought. *Only more so.*

142

"Sit down. Take off your coats."

They did. A man's sweater hung over an armchair. A few stale cigars were crumpled into a big marble ashtray. Abigail Robbins sat in a high-backed bentwood rocker across from Ryker and Christie. She rocked and sipped what looked like straight scotch. Her skin, from her pink toes to her barely covered thighs, was smooth and opaque like milk glass. Long, straight strawberry blond hair hung down to her breasts. The short white kimono peeked open every time she rocked. Christie stared. She wasn't wearing any underwear at all, he realized. He squirmed in his seat.

"Drink?"

"Later."

"What can I do for you?" She popped a lozenge in her mouth.

Let me fuck you and fuck you, Christie thought.

"Well," Ryker said, "this is a volunteer-type assignment—okay?"

"Okay."

"Okay, do you volunteer?"

"What's the assignment?"

"None of my men would have the balls to ask me that."

"I'm not one of your men, Sergeant."

"This is an undercover job," Ryker said. "A deep penetration."

All the way past your cervix and into your uterus, if I can get it that far, Christie thought.

"Mafia? Terrorists?"

"No. A witches' coven."

"A what?"

"Witches' coven. That's a group of witches. Usually thirteen—"

"Oh, the Mad Monk case?"

"You have a quick mind," Ryker said.

"Don't fuck me around, please. I'm not feeling well."

"I have a good doctor I'd like you to see, then."

"Who?"

"Dr. Morlock."

"He's an M.E. I'm not that sick. I mean, I don't want my death certificate to read, 'Cause of death: Autopsy.'" She laughed.

Christie's heart paused when she laughed. He was in love.

"He's a witch. A warlock."

"No shit?"

"No shit."

"He eats cadavers?"

"I don't know. That's his business. We're going over there now. Want to come?"

She hesitated. "Well . . ."

Christie spoke up. "Look, you have to know about these covens first. At the Grand Sabbats—you know what that is. . . ."

"Yeah, I know about them."

"Yeah, well, they have these Black Masses, and well, after these Black Masses they . . ."

"Have orgies. I know. They fuck and suck."

"Yeah. Right. Well . . . ?"

"Will one or both of you be along?"

"One of us will be with you," Ryker said.

"Who would the lucky son of a bitch be if I agreed to this?"

"Would that affect your decision?" Ryker asked, before his partner could speak.

"No. I think you're both equally disgusting." She smiled.

Christie's heart stopped again. It stopped every time she smiled.

"Come with us to Morlock's. We'll fill you in on the way," Ryker said.

"Wait a minute. I feel like I'm being hustled. There's a lot of AC/DC swapping at orgies, right? How do I know I won't wind up with some sixty-year-old bull dyke all over me?"

That reminded Christie again of getting buggered by some warlock; it was still a good question.

Ryker looked at her hard. "It's a Village coven. All young people, according to Julia Preston, the surviving victim. Would you mind a young fem type all over you? What about an eighteen-year-old punk shit? What can you put up with? What have you already done?"

She looked back at Ryker. "That's my business."

"Well, you'll have to stick very close to each other if you want to avoid that, then."

"It's Christie who will be my partner, then?" She looked a little disappointed.

Ryker caught the look and filed it away for future reference. "Right."

She crossed her long legs and looked at Peter Christie. "You look young. I don't want a morals rap hanging over my head." She laughed again, then rolled the lozenge around in her mouth and slid down deeper into the rocker. She looked very cool. Christie wanted to knock Ryker over the head and rape her, but he said nothing.

"Okay, let's go then," Ryker said. "I want to catch Morlock before he jumps on a broomstick and flies off."

"You want to call?"

"No. I called his doorman before. He's expected back from work at six. It's after six now. This will be a 'what an unexpected pleasure'-type visit."

"All right. I'm willing to listen, anyway." She jumped abruptly out of her chair. "Turn around or stand in the stove or something. I'll get dressed."

The two cops got up and walked over to the door.

Abigail Robbins quickly stepped into a pair of panties and jeans. She slipped a turtleneck sweater over her full, bare breasts.

"Why don't you buy a goddamned screen so your guests don't have to stand with their noses to the wall?" Ryker asked.

"I don't usually care who sees me get dressed," she said, pulling on a pair of boots.

"I've heard." Ryker couldn't resist the line.

"Look," she said. "I don't need any shit from you, Ryker. You come over here asking me to fuck for the cause and you expect to find a twenty-four-year-old virgin sitting on a rocker knitting socks for the Orphan's Relief Fund."

"You're going to make a good witch," Ryker said. "You're only a hop, step, and a jump away from one already."

"Come on," Christie pleaded. "No more fighting."

"Just a lovers' quarrel," Robbins said. She grabbed a long raccoon coat, and walked past Ryker and Christie as if they were of no more interest to her than a couple of plastic garbage bags filled with shit.

ELEVEN

"What an unexpected pleasure," Dr. Morlock said smoothly. "Come in, please."

Ryker introduced Abigail Robbins, then the three cops followed the old doctor down the long hall.

"Jesus Christ . . . look at this place," Robbins whispered.

"You ain't seen nothing yet," Christie whispered back.

When they came into the large bloodred chamber, Morlock swung around.

"Take off your coats. Please sit down." A man, perhaps the butler, appeared behind them and took their things.

Ryker, startled, figured there must be a hidden door in that hallway. It was the second time someone had been able to sneak up behind him in this apartment. He didn't like it.

The three cops took separate black-shrouded armchairs around a large coffee table. Morlock remained standing.

"Can I get you all a drink?" He smiled and turned

to Christie. "Or are you still afraid to drink anything in my house, young man?"

Christie reddened. "Bloody Mary," he said. "Real blood."

"I'll see what I can do," Morlock said suavely. "Sergeant Ryker? Miss Robbins?"

"Bourbon on the rocks."

"Scotch on the rocks."

The butler nodded and moved off. Morlock sat. He was wearing a black dressing gown again, and in the dim light, he blended into the black chair.

"What an interesting room," Robbins said with a smile. "Did you see this in *Better Homes and Gardens?*"

Morlock just smiled back. Ryker said conversationally, "How's your nephew? Not too much of a pain in the ass, I hope."

Morlock caught the reference.

"He's gone home," Morlock said evenly.

"Doctor," Ryker began formally, "as I suspected, we're going to need your help again."

"Sergeant, I've helped you all I can. If I hear of anything else that might be of assistance to you in this case, as I said, I will call you."

"Yeah, Doc. Right. But we need some expert advice now."

"Such as?"

"My young friends here are going to join a coven. They want some background on what to do and say. How to act. You know, the whole bit."

"I see. Which coven?"

"We'll just keep that under our cowls for now, okay, Doc?"

"Fine. I suspect it is the coven that those two unfortunate girls belonged to, though."

The drinks came.

"No mind-reading, please." Ryker emptied his

148

glass in one long pull and slammed it on the coffee table. The butler gave a little jump, then retrieved the empty glass and disappeared with it.

"How will their joining a coven help you find this monk?"

"We'll tell you later when we tell you which coven."

"All right, but you can trust me completely. I told you, I'm as anxious to see him caught as you are."

"Yeah. I remember we discussed it. How did your seance work out, by the way?"

"I was going to call you today about that. Unfortunately, it turned out not as well as we had hoped." The doctor sipped his yellowish drink.

The butler returned and placed a half-full bottle of I. W. Harper and a glass in front of Ryker.

"That's a pity," Ryker said, pouring four fingers of bourbon in his glass.

"Sure is," Christie added, examining his drink. "We were counting pretty heavy on that seance."

"I'm sure." Morlock licked his small, bloodless lips. "It doesn't always work as well as we would like. The adept, while he was projected to the astral level, did sense something that perhaps would be of use to you, however."

"Sure. Shoot," Ryker said, leaning back in the black armchair.

Robbins looked around at the men. This was getting weirder.

"Well, the adept," Morlock began with his eyes closed, "sensed the presence of an evil spirit between two closely flowing rivers." His voice was dreamy and far away. "This led us to deduce that the monk was on the island of Manhattan. Presumably downtown, where the Hudson and East Rivers are separated by a short distance. The sun was rising, though, so it is on the East Side. South of Fourteenth Street, I should say. In your precinct, probably. That's all we got."

Ryker kept his expressionless eyes fixed on Morlock, thinking angrily that somebody leaked the old fuck the information.

"Was that any help, Sergeant?" Morlock was still smiling.

"When I find out who fed you that, I'll have both your balls bronzed."

"I beg your pardon?"

"Okay, let's get down to business. How long will it take to get these two briefed to join a coven?"

Morlock looked thoughtful. "Well, will it be a robed initiation or a sky-clad initiation?"

"How the hell should I know? I don't know what the fuck you're talking about." Ryker was getting impatient.

"I'm sorry. I assumed you were familiar with the coven these two initiates are going to join."

"Does it make a difference?"

"No. I can teach them both initiation rituals, and enough background to get by at a meeting. Does this coven have regular meetings, by the way?"

"Yes," Ryker answered. "Friday nights."

"Of course. Friday nights."

"Of course," Robbins said. "Everybody knows that. What's the difference in initiations? I can probably guess anyway."

"Yes?" Morlock said smoothly. "The robed one, as the name implies, is done clad in robes. The sky-clad is done naked, of course."

"Of course," Robbins said.

"I'll take the sky-clad!" Christie said.

Morlock looked up. "I'm afraid that's not for me to decide, young man. This is not *my* coven you're joining."

"Right." Christie was red.

"You know," Morlock said thoughtfully, "if I

150

wasn't being blackmailed into doing this, I wouldn't be doing it. This is a very serious business, Sergeant Ryker, and I'm afraid at least one of your young friends is not very serious about it. I doubt if either is."

"Look, Doc," Ryker said. "Maybe they'll get serious and become good witches later. If it's any consolation to you, it *is* a Greenwich Village coven that they're going to join. Those people are not very serious to begin with, are they? That's what you said."

"Yes, that is true. Well, if it's any consolation to *you*, Mr. Christie, if it is the Greenwich Village coven, I'm quite positive it will be a sky-clad initiation," Morlock said, taking a sip of his drink. "I still feel that I'm not doing the right thing, however. This is wrong—"

"Look," Ryker interrupted, "nobody can accuse you of selling your soul to the Devil—you've already done that."

Robbins laughed.

"We have a common goal here. Let's get on the stick, okay?"

"All right." Morlock sighed. "I have two more preparatory questions."

"Shoot."

"Do you know if this coven will perform the ritual of initiation at the Esbat?"

"Who?"

"The Esbat. That's the weekly or fortnightly Friday meeting."

"Fortnightly?" Christie asked.

"That's every two weeks, idiot," Ryker snapped. "No. I don't know—why?"

"Well, my group, for instance, will only do the initiation on one of the Grand Sabbats."

"Oh."

"But it's all right. Most covens will carry you along until then. You can attend all the Esbats until the initiation at the Sabbat at Walpurgis Night. On the other hand, I think this group will do the initiation right away at an Esbat. They're impatient children, and they won't wait for the Sabbat. They enjoy doing the initiation. If it's sky-clad, I'm sure you'll enjoy it also." He looked at the two young cops. "Which brings me to my next question. Miss Robbins? Mr. Christie?"

They both looked alert.

"Are either of you very religious?"

"Why?"

Morlock settled back. "Well, the initiation, even if done naked, is rather a mild ceremony compared to the Grand Sabbats. Now the Esbats, or Friday-night meetings, are just that—meetings. But the Grand Sabbats—now that's another story."

"We know," Christie said.

"Like hell we do," Robbins said. "Give me a briefing, please."

"Well . . ." Morlock looked at the pretty woman. "They are Black Masses, followed by what you would call an orgy."

"That's what I call it," Robbins said.

"Yes. Well, the orgy might not even be as difficult for you as the Black Mass itself."

"Why?" Abigail Robbins looked concerned.

"Do you have any religious affiliations? In which of the heresies were you raised?"

"Heresies?"

"Churches," Morlock said distastefully.

"Oh. I'm a Catholic," Robbins said.

"I see. Well, the Black Mass is a parody of the Christian mass, basically the Catholic mass. The name of your Lord God is definitely taken in vain.

The cross is hung upside down. There will be distasteful pictures of naked saints. Sometimes there will be a naked statue of Mary. There may be a Christ with a large penis; you may have to kiss it and—"

"Hold on there, Morlock," Robbins said, standing up. "This is sick."

"Not at all," Morlock said. "It's our religion. Yours too, if—"

"Bullshit."

"Sit down," Ryker said. His voice was like a hammer.

"Don't bully me."

Christie saw the plan coming apart again. "Please."

"You don't give a rat's ass, Ryker," she said. "You don't have to do it."

"If you wanted to pound a typewriter in the fucking steno pool, why did you become a detective?" Ryker sneered.

"I didn't ask for *this*."

"I'm sure you've done worse. I thought you were looking forward to the orgy."

"Like hell. I can get laid without it, which is more than I can say for you three."

"Please. Please." Christie was standing between them now.

Morlock sat back and locked his fingers together. He was smiling.

"Forget it!" Ryker bellowed. "Just forget it. Miss Pussy Willow here wants to see more people butchered. Okay, forget it. Let the men handle it."

Abigail Robbins turned her back on the group. She stood silently. After a minute, she turned around. She walked up to Ryker and looked directly into his eyes. "Tell me to my face that this is the only way," she said in a low voice. "Tell me you have no other leads. Tell me no one else will volunteer for this."

The two cops stared into each other's eyes.

"There's no other way," Ryker said slowly. "No other leads," he lied. "We asked everyone else. We need *you.*" If there had been a polygraph attached to him as he spoke, it would have shorted a fuse. Ryker never moved a facial muscle.

She looked deep into his burning green eyes and sighed. "Okay. Let's get the fucking show on the road."

Morlock gave the cops a preliminary briefing about the best way to approach a coven. Reluctantly, he agreed to act as the sponsor. He carried a lot of weight even among the Greenwich Village crowd because he contributed small amounts of money from time to time to the poorer covens, even if they *were* made up of children. He asked the two young cops to call on him during the week for a more detailed explanation of the rites.

Ryker told Morlock how they intended to entrap the monk.

"This sounds dangerous to the coven," Morlock said.

Ryker was squeezing the last drops out of the I. W. Harper bottle. "Not at all," he lied. "There will be plenty of back-up people there."

"I still don't approve of this method."

"Is that so? Well, you're going to approve of it even less when I tell you that I'm joining your little group for the April 30 Sabbat."

"What for?" The frail-looking old man seemed panicky.

"There are going to be two notices placed in the papers and magazines. Your Walpurgis Night Sabbat will be one of them."

"No."

"Yes."

Christie had been wondering when his partner was going to spring this on the old warlock. For a while he had thought perhaps Ryker had changed his mind about it. He should have known better. Robbins looked at Ryker with a smile of approval. She hadn't known about this, either.

"You'll introduce me as an accomplished warlock. I don't feel like going through a fucking initiation."

"No. You don't understand what goes on at a Grand Sabbat. Sometimes—"

"I understand well enough," Ryker said. "You fuck young boys. You practice all types of sexual deviation. You probably use drugs, too. I'm not on the vice squad or the narcotics squad. I couldn't care less how you get your jollies."

"We can't have it," Morlock said, shaking his head. "We simply can't have it."

"Look," Ryker said, "I'll be alone. No partner— okay? The back-up men will be on the street. You have my word—no trouble with the police."

"But the ad will attract other witches—perhaps people who are not witches," Morlock protested. "This is a very exclusive coven. There will be a lot of prominent people there for a Grand Sabbat. Recognizable people."

"You rich fucks make me sick. Even your witches' covens are full of snobs. How do you stomach each other?"

"We manage."

"Look, I'm sure everyone at these things are so fucking prominent that they must come incognito, right?"

Morlock hesitated. "Yes. Yes, that's true. They wear masks."

"How about their names?"

"They only use their witches' names, but their voices are recognizable in some cases. We can't have outsiders here."

"Then tell them to keep their mouths shut."

Morlock was desperate. "It simply won't work. If this monk shows up here, his arrest will be all over the papers. It will be a tremendous scandal."

"You witches are like everybody else. You don't want to get involved. Listen, chances are one in a thousand that he will come here first, if at all. He'll hit the Village first if he sees that ad. The address is an old church rectory. That'll piss him off enough to make him want to go there. He may even hit a weekly Esbat there before April 30. This place is only a back-up for the Sabbat—get it? Anyway, I'll instruct my men to make the arrest in the street or the lobby before he ever gets up here. He's hard to miss. You won't be involved. Anyway, you have no choice, know what I mean?"

Ryker didn't even know what he meant, but long ago he'd learned that vague threats were the best. Everyone had something to hide. You didn't even have to know *what* in order to make a threat.

Morlock nodded his head slowly.

"You're being very cooperative, Doctor," Ryker said. "We're going to put you in for the Mayor's Citizenship Medal."

"Don't bother, please."

"One more thing."

"What?"

"We need a layout for those announcements. A real good ad that will bring in the customers. But we want it obscure enough so that only the real witches will notice it. We don't want a mob scene here or at the Village location. It has to be in words only a few will understand. And don't worry about the CPM."

"The what?"

"Forget it."

Morlock looked down sadly. At length he called for some paper, pens, a ruler, and a compass. He went to work and a half hour later pushed the finished product across the coffee table toward Ryker. Christie and Robbins were wandering around the big room. They sat down.

Ryker looked at it. It was a large circle that closely resembled the circle of the Zodiac. Strange, curling characters were written in the margins. "Well, it's obscure enough," he said. "What the fuck is it?"

"It's a witch's wheel. Much like a zodiac wheel. I have an arrow pointing to the Festival of Walpurgis Night. The writing is in witch's runes. They give the addresses of the two Sabbats. The time is always midnight, of course, so I didn't put it in. In addition, I've mentioned the weekly Esbats at the Village location. It also says only solitary witches with no existing covens are invited to the festival."

"Sort of like a Salvation Army Christmas party for the down-and-out, huh, Doc?"

"That's what you're turning this Sabbat into," Morlock said. "Witches are not known for their charity even amongst other witches."

"A little Christian charity would do us all a world of good," Ryker said, smiling.

"Please!" Morlock said. "Don't use that word."

The three cops held back their laughter.

Morlock rose. "May I ask you what you think will happen when this Village coven, not to mention my own, sees that thing in the papers or magazines?"

"Good question. You will explain to your people ahead of time. Make up some story about wanting to expand the coven. After Christie and Robbins penetrate this Village coven under your sponsorship, you will contact this group and offer to supply the money for free eats and stuff if they will open their coven to stray witches. This will explain the ad if they see it. Tell them you're trying to spread the faith. They'll bite."

"You're pretty free with my money."

"The Special Operations Fund is a little short this month."

Morlock paced around the room. "I have another question."

"Shoot."

"Why don't you just run the ad without the real addresses? Use policemen to play the parts. They can just sit around and play poker until the monk arrives. It would be a lot safer for us."

Ryker leaned back in his chair. "I thought of that, Doc. There's a lot to be said for both ways of doing it. In the end, though, it's like this: First, I want it to look as real as possible. This guy may be crazy, but he's no dummy. Second, it takes time, money, and people to keep up a front like this. You have to have people coming and going, in addition to the back-up. If he doesn't hit on April 30 or at a weekly meeting, then we have to keep up the front addresses until the Summer Solstice Sabbat on June 21, then Lammas Night on August 1, then Halloween. Too expensive."

Ryker paused, then continued. "We're going over to that Village church later to have a look-see. Also, the monk, if he checks, can see that they have these weekly Esbats regularly. Christie and Robbins will be at each one once they join this coven. If the monk changes his MO and decides to hit one of these Friday-night meetings, we'll be waiting for him. We'll have a back-up team there each Friday. It has to look like a legitimate coven—get it? Anyway, we have a jury to consider after we make an arrest. It will look much better this way. Mad Monk attacks Greenwich Village coven."

"What if he attacks *mine?*"

"You should be happy to help. We're doing it for you, right? I mean this is not your run-of-the-mill murderer. He kills only witches."

"That first girl wasn't a witch," Morlock pointed out. "Nor are the next victims likely to be if he keeps killing actresses who play witches."

"Correct," Ryker conceded. "But his heart's in the right place. He just gets confused. That's why we're trying to steer him in the right direction."

"I don't find that amusing."

"Well, the point is, we want to use that Village coven as bait. Your place here is only a back-up. I think he'll go for the Village first." Ryker picked up the ad Morlock had written and studied it. "Do you think he can read this runic shit? I wanted Latin."

"Latin!" Morlock said, laughing. "That's the Christian church's language. It wouldn't be very believable."

"Yeah, but he's a monk—real or phony."

"Let him learn runic letters if he doesn't know them. He can translate this with any book on witchcraft, or he can go to the library once he realizes what it is."

"Okay, you're the witch. This guy has a name, by the way: Zachariah."

"Zachariah," Morlock repeated. "'One who is remembered by Jehovah.' That's the Hebrew translation."

"They don't make names like that anymore." Ryker stood. His partners followed. "Okay, Doc. That's about it. For tonight."

The three cops put on their coats. At the door,

Ryker turned to Morlock. "This isn't the first time I've been in league with the Devil, and it probably won't be the last."

"You could do worse," Morlock said, with an evil smile.

"Not much."

TWELVE

The three cops walked west to Fifth Avenue and stood in the cold waiting for a cab to take them south to Washington Square Park. It was past seven P.M.

"I'm going to get pneumonia," Robbins said, sniffling.

"You'll live," Ryker said absently. His mind was going over the events of the last forty hours or so since he was summoned to Barrow Street at four in the morning. It seemed to him that Zachariah was covered from all angles. Lindly would post the men at Lincoln Center on April 30, and he would cover some other theaters whose productions might attract the monk. Littel was in charge of canvassing the precinct, house by house. He, Ryker, was setting up a baited trap. Two baited traps. Of the three prongs of the attack, his seemed least likely to succeed, but it was certainly the most fun. He smiled to himself.

"How did that shithead Morlock know about Zach's address?" Christie asked. "Do you really think he got that from . . . astral . . . What do you call it?"

"Grow up," Ryker said harshly.

THE HAMMER OF GOD

"You mean Morlock's information about the location of the monk was accurate?" Robbins asked.

Christie explained briefly how they had gotten their lead.

"Sounds scary," she said. "If he doesn't have a source in the department . . ."

"He has a source, somebody big," Ryker said. "There's no such fucking thing as astral projection, period."

They discussed Morlock for the next several minutes. They were impressed with this strange man in spite of themselves. The conversation drifted back to the plan at hand.

"You know," Christie said, waving frantically at an off-duty cab. "This is a harebrained scheme. Even if we do suck the monk into the trap, Morlock was right. It's dangerous to a lot of innocent people. We should use a front address."

"Why?"

"I told you—it's safer."

"Look," Ryker said. "I have other reasons for wanting to penetrate one of these witches' covens besides Zachariah."

"Like what?"

"You heard Morlock say that there would be a lot of VIP's at his Sabbat," Ryker said. "I figured there would be. Well, I'd like nothing better than to be able to identify a few of these fat cats. I'd like to have my fingers wrapped around their balls in case I ever need one of them in a pinch someday. That's called developing clout and leverage. You have to cover your ass on this job."

"Sounds like blackmail to me," Robbins said.

"Not unless my back is up against the wall. It's nice to have a friend if you need one. When you've been on the job almost twenty years, you'll understand that." Ryker smiled into the darkness.

162

Finally, they got a cab and rode in silence downtown.

Ryker thought about Morlock's "seance." For a wild moment he thought that maybe Morlock did get his lead through occult means. It was not completely unknown. The Lindbergh kidnapping case had used a seer of some sort to try to locate the kidnapped baby, he remembered. There had been other cases since then in the annals of police work. After some deep thought, he dismissed the possibility as a lot of trash. He would have to find Morlock's source among the thirty or so detectives on his squad. There were also others at One Police Plaza who had access to the same information. Was it possible that some cop was a practicing witch? Another headache.

The cab stopped at the end of Fifth Avenue near the Washington Square arch. The three cops got out and began walking through the deserted park. They turned west and left the area of numbered streets behind, walking the twisting, winding streets of the Village. Many of these streets had been laid out in the seventeenth and eighteenth centuries. Some of the buildings went back almost that far; others were new or renovated. The days of the quaint, cheap little apartment in the Village were long over. The area was expensive, chic, and very gay.

On Charles Street, not too far from the murder scene at Barrow Street, they stopped in front of a complex of deserted church buildings once known as St. Jude's. During the 60s, the church had sold the complex to a builder who was going to put up a high-rise condo, but the builder had gone broke and sold the property to an enterprising rich kid named Randolff, who promptly built a disco there. The disco became famous and Randolff went to jail for tax evasion. It later became a club featuring punk-rock and New Wave bands, until finally, the State Liquor Authority closed it down.

The former church complex was now scheduled for demolition; the land was just too valuable to remain idle and unproductive for long. In the meantime, the coven had decided the rectory would make the perfect spot for their services-cum-orgies. If the current owners had known that a bunch of kids were using the property, they would have hired dogs and guards. But they were blissfully ignorant and saving some money while they were busy wining and dining city officials to get the necessary demolition and building permits.

At the rear of the church stood the small rectory building; the windows were lit by moonlight. Christie swore he saw figures pass to and fro behind the windows, but Ryker pointed out that it was only the clouds passing in front of the moon that gave the illusion of an occupied building.

Ryker pushed the dry bushes aside and discovered a stairway that led to the cellar entrance. Christie touched the heavy .38 Police Special in his shoulder holster for the fourth or fifth time. Ryker shouldered through the bushes and went down the stone steps. A heavy oak door stood at the end of the stairwell. Ryker lit a match. A sign nailed to the door read: NO TRESPASSING. His two partners came up behind him quietly. Christie produced a small penlight so Ryker could examine the huge padlock. He sorted through his passkeys while Christie held the shaking light. Robbins was sneezing.

"Hold the fucking light still," Ryker said.

"I'm cold," Christie said.

"You're scared," Robbins said.

"Bullshit."

The lock suddenly snapped open in Ryker's hand. He pushed on the heavy black door. It swung open with an eerie creak; a rat scurried across the floor a few yards from his feet. The three cops fanned out and crouched low, guns drawn. Ryker didn't expect anyone to be home, but precautions were something you took like you took a breath. When you stopped taking precautions, it was like when you stopped breathing —you died.

Christie snapped on the penlight again. A small but powerful beam reached the far wall. The basement was a single room about twenty by fifty feet. The penlight traveled across the massive stone blocks of the foundation and floor which had been built before the age of poured concrete. Water glistened on them in the light of the small beam; the air smelled of fungus and mildew.

Ryker walked toward the middle of the room, where a tall black candle sat on a stack of bricks. He touched a match to it and looked around. The room, within the circle of light, was almost empty except for a few odds and ends that obviously pertained to the witches' meetings.

Spokes of a wheel, drawn in white chalk, radiated from the stack of bricks and disappeared into the dark recesses of the room. Ryker realized that the bricks and candle were the altar.

"They should see how the other half lives at Morlock's," Ryker said. His voice echoed through the cold, damp cellar. Robbins sneezed again.

"Still wish you were sitting on some dull beach in Spain?" Ryker said to Christie.

"Fucking right I do."

"Pussy," Ryker said.

"Pussy," Robbins said.

"Get off my back, you two."

The three cops looked around from their circle of light. Finally Ryker said, "There're more candles, but I don't want to light them. In fact, I think we've disturbed the place enough already. Let's get the hell out of here." He snuffed out the black candle, and led the way toward the door.

On the path leading to the street, Ryker stopped and took out a notebook. He began making a rough sketch of the church grounds.

"I wanted to get you two oriented so you wouldn't see this place for the first time when you get initiated," he said.

"Let's look around some more," Robbins said.

Ryker looked up from his drawing. "You two go ahead. I'll finish this map. See if there's someplace a man could hide in the church compound."

Christie shrugged. They were both nuts, he decided. He vaulted over the low stone wall; Robbins followed. The moon was setting and the frozen turf crackled under their feet as they walked cautiously through the deserted churchyard.

"Isn't this romantic?" Robbins said.

"Whatever turns you on," Christie replied. "Look, let me get you home before you're really sick."

"Don't worry about it."

Christie was annoyed. "I don't know who's more of a hard-ass, you or Ryker."

"When are *you* going to start being a hard-ass?"

"Don't give me that crap."

"Well?"

Christie felt like bragging. "We got the lead on Zachariah's address because I beat the shit out of those two guys."

"I thought Ryker said they were kids."

She turned around and began walking back. Christie fell into step beside her.

"You kicked the small one in the balls."

"The big one. They were dangerous people," Christie said. "One of them had a meat cleaver."

"*You* had the meat cleaver. That's what Ryker said while we were waiting for a cab, remember?"

"He was just trying to make a small thing of my bravery in action. He's jealous."

"I'm not impressed."

"Who cares?"

"You do. Look, Ryker brought us here so we'd be familiar with the layout," she said.

I'd like to get familiar with your layout, he thought. "A little orientation and terrain appreciation, I think they call it."

"Right," she said. Then she laughed. "You're going to see something else tonight for the first time so that you're not surprised at the initiation."

Christie felt his mouth go dry.

"What?" He knew.

"Me. A little orientation and terrain appreciation. My place—later. We might as well get this over with."

"Don't put yourself out." His heart was beating rapidly.

"No trouble. I don't want you going ape-shit at the initiation. You have to look cool. Also, at the Sabbat orgy in April, if we make it that far, I want you to stick close, if you'll pardon the pun. I want to be screwed by as few people as possible. We'll start learning how to stick close tonight." She began walking again. "The things I do for my paycheck," she sighed.

Christie walked in silence, then said, "You'd rather have Ryker with you, wouldn't you?"

"He's a little too mature for this coven."

"Answer the question."

"I'd rather be in the typing pool."

"Forget it, then. Don't do me any favors."

She took his arm. "Come on. I'm cold."

They rejoined Ryker, who was smoking a cigar as he scanned the buildings.

The three frozen cops walked to the busy center of the Village, found a small Italian restaurant, and drank cups of espresso laced with anisette. As they talked quietly for the next hour, Ryker could sense a strain between his two young partners. He figured correctly that they had come to some sort of understanding and that they would probably spend the night in the same bed. He looked at Christie.

"You're on special duty tonight. The house-to-house, remember?"

Christie had forgotten.

"Look, I'm sort of beat. I mean, couldn't I . . ."

"Sure," Ryker said. "I can reach you at home tonight if anything comes up, then?"

"Well, yeah."

Ryker called for the bill, Robbins insisted on paying, and they left. Ryker decided to walk home, while the two young cops caught a cab uptown.

"How 'bout my place instead?" Christie said when they reached the East Side.

"Whatever," Robbins said.

Dog-tired and feeling queasy, Ryker trudged wearily across town, sucking in the frigid air, trying to make himself feel better. He was wondering if he had done the right thing exposing the two young cops to a potentially dangerous situation. *No,* he thought, *that's what they're paid for—not to play it safe.*

The other thing he wondered, as he walked up the stairs to his empty apartment, was if he should have made it with Abigail Robbins. She was obviously willing; he was interested, too. It had been a long time since he had screwed a nonprofessional. *They were softer, less sure, more of a challenge,* he thought. But they always wanted something in return—something he wasn't willing to give. Also, he didn't want to get young Christie pissed off. *Let 'em fuck each other blue,* he thought. *They've got work to do. And so do I.*

On the fifth-floor landing, he collided with a huge,

soft mound of flesh. It was the biker, Wolf, lying in front of his door like a one-faced Mt. Rushmore.

"Get up, you asshole," Ryker said, nudging the huge man with his foot. "Out of my way."

"Zat you, Ryker?" Wolf mumbled.

"No, it's the fucking meter maid. You're parked in front of my goddamn door."

"They robbed me, Ryker," he said in his high, whistling whine. "They took my hawg."

"Good."

"No, listen, ya gotta help me get her back."

"I don't gotta do anything, asshole," Ryker said, "except kick the shit out of you."

"Please, Ryker," the biker shrilled, struggling to get his massive bulk off the floor.

The phone was ringing inside Ryker's apartment.

"Call me tomorrow," Ryker said, shoving the now-upright Wolf out of his way and unlocking the door.

"Now, Ryker," the biker pleaded.

"Tomorrow," Ryker said, spinning around, and throwing his left forearm into the biker's monstrous belly. The air blew out of Wolf's lungs with a whoosing sound, and he went down with a crash. Ryker slammed the door and lurched for the phone. He heard Eleanor's voice say, "I guess he's not home," before she hung up.

"Bastard," Ryker said, slamming the receiver down. He had really wanted to talk to Ellie tonight, but when he called her apartment and her office, no one answered.

THIRTEEN

The week passed quickly. All systems were in full swing. The full effort of the department pressed heavily toward Zachariah.

On Friday morning, detectives Procino and Ward walked into the derelict building on Third Street and Avenue D. They knocked on a few doors at random, but no one was home or no one wanted to answer. Finally, on the second floor, they found a brave soul and flashed their tin.

Procino pulled the artist's sketch from his pocket. "This man live here?"

An old man looked at the two detectives.

"You speak English, Pop?"

"*Sí*. Small English."

"Small English. Great. This man, he lives here?"

The old man looked down at the picture. He hesitated. "No. I no see him."

Procino looked at the old man. "You know everybody in this building?"

"No."

"You know anybody in the building?"

170

"No."

"Then how do you know he doesn't live here?"

Señor, I see this man, I know it pretty quick."

Procino laughed. "Let's keep banging on doors and get it over with."

Ward nodded. For the tenth time that morning, they began climbing stairs. On each floor they picked a few apartments and knocked. The tenants who answered were shown the picture. Everyone had more or less the same comment. "If I ever saw that face, I wouldn't forget it."

Procino was frustrated. "How the hell can he disappear like this?" he said.

"Nobody can hide so good that nobody in their building has ever seen them," Ward said.

"I suppose." He counted the doors on one floor. Fifteen. All single rooms. Six floors. Ninety single room apartments. Weekly and monthly rentals. Communal kitchen and toilets. They knocked on more doors. On the fifth floor, Zachariah stood with his big head pressed against the door. The knock on his door reverberated through the thin wood and bounced his head slightly. He tightened his grip on the handle of a big double-headed ax. The knock came again; then fading footsteps. Another knock further down the hall.

"Yes?"

"Police—open up."

A door opened.

"Ever see this man?"

Silence.

"Well?"

"Hell, no. He's weird." A deep male voice.

"Who lives there in C-12?"

"Can't say. I got here last week."

"Okay. If you see this man, please call this number.

He's dangerous. Take this card. Name's Procino, but talk to any detective there, okay?"

"Sure."

Footsteps. Another knock, further away. The cops passed out about twenty-seven cards in a building of ninety apartments. They felt satisfied; they had no pangs of conscience as they checked the building off their list. There were a lot more to go. They would double back this way before April 30 if they had the time. Maybe someone would spot the monk and remember the card. Maybe someone would call.

Zachariah walked quietly over to his night table. He put the ax on the floor, then poured a large measure of wine into a wooden goblet and drank. He picked up a bit of moldy cheese and chewed absently. The cheese crumbs stuck in his full black beard. He poured another goblet of wine and sat on his bed slats. Something, he knew, had gone wrong. Was it because he was so evil?

He *was* evil. He knew that with the certainty born of complete faith in a merciful God. No matter how hard he tried, Zachariah could never quite erase the memory of his twelfth summer.

He had been big for his age. He had always been big, as far back as he could remember. Big and evil. His mother had always told him so. She had whipped him for every indiscretion, for every mistake, and even if he tried his hardest to be good, he was whipped for harboring evil thoughts.

The evil thoughts had become unbearable his twelfth summer. The lust he felt in his loins was like a living thing, taking possession of him, leading him down the path of unrighteousness. His mother knew this, and the beatings increased in both intensity and frequency.

He could remember standing naked and ashamed before his mother, his organ erect and ludicrous, swaying in front of him. She had screamed and beaten him until his buttocks had bled freely. It felt good; she was beating the Devil out of him. He would be godly from then on. He swore it.

Then a month later, his cousin Rachel came to visit. She was intoxicating. Older than Zachariah by four years, she was worldly and kind. She talked to him as an adult and seemed genuinely interested in him and his innermost thoughts. Within a week he was hopelessly in love with her, little realizing she was a blasphemous witch; that he was in love with Evil.

It happened on a sweltering August night. He was sweaty and restless, confined by the flannel nightshirt his mother insisted he wear summer and winter. In an act of rebellion, he stripped it off and lay naked on top of the covers, thinking about Rachel. It happened, as it happened in his wicked dreams, but this time it was real. Rachel came to him, wearing the nightdress she always wore. He could see her firm, upthrusting breasts and bright pink nipples through the thin material. His eyes went automatically to the dark, mysterious thatch between her legs. He groaned.

She came to him, her full lips on his, her tongue probing the depths of his mouth, her hand resting lightly on his hairless chest. Then her mouth left his and traveled down his chest; her tongue caressed his nipples a moment before moving lower. His penis was fully erect, painful; he was trembling with desire, shaking with lust as her cool mouth took his hot organ inside. It took only a few seconds before his seed exploded inside her mouth—at exactly the same time his mother snapped on the light.

"Witch!" she screamed. "Evil, filthy slut! Release my son!"

Zachariah trembled at the harsh sound of his mother's voice; he cringed in humiliation and terror. The witch had seduced him—an innocent boy—and must be killed. They must all die, so that Good could live and flourish.

He ran his meaty hand over the curved blade of his double-headed ax.

"Dear God, they shall all pay with their lives, so that their souls may be free." It was a prayer, a pledge, a certainty.

"No, I'm not sure," Ryker said to Lieutenant Fischetti as they sat in the deserted conference room. "I'm not sure at all, but it has to be done."

"It's semi-illegal," Fischetti said. He was worried, as usual.

"The monk is more than semi-dangerous, and that's the point. We've got to snatch the bastard off the street before he goes into his act again," Ryker said, lighting a cigar. It was almost eight P.M. The Esbat in Greenwich Village was due to begin in a few hours, and Fischetti was jumpy. He and Ryker had been talking for almost thirty minutes; they weren't getting anywhere.

"I've got to get out of here and set up the surveillance," Ryker said. It was pointless to continue the conversation.

Just then, Detective Littel stuck his head in the door and told Ryker he had a phone call. "It's your wife, I think," Littel said. "Sounds like she is real upset. She's lost her pet pig."

"Her what?" Ryker said, punching the blinking light on the phone. "Eleanor, what the hell's wrong?"

Silence.

"Eleanor? What is it?"

"This is Wolf," the high-pitched voice said. "About my hawg, my bike, man, you know."

"Oh, for Christssakes, get off the line, you asshole," Ryker said, slamming the receiver into the cradle.

"Nice way to talk to your wife," Fischetti said. "No wonder she divorced you."

"Fuck off, Lieutenant," Ryker said. "I'm leaving."

"The poor woman loses her pet pig and you're no help at all," Fischetti said, shaking his head.

"I'm her pet pig," Ryker said, slamming the door.

Christie called on Abigail Robbins at her apartment at nine P.M. that evening. He felt like a kid on his first date despite having slept with this date earlier in the week. It seemed to him that both of them had enjoyed the sex, but she hadn't asked him to come over again. He had asked her and had gotten an evasive answer, so they spent their days doing routine police work.

Each night, they went together to Morlock's for a witchcraft briefing. Morlock assured them that they were ready for the initiation. He had contacted Professor Weirman of the Village coven during the week. Weirman and his high priestess, it seemed, were the only older members of the coven. Christie and Robbins listened in on an extension as Morlock spoke with Weirman. The professor seemed pleased to hear from so august a witch as Dr. Morlock, but Morlock didn't like what he had heard about Weirman. He suspected that the middle-aged professor started this coven for his own personal sexual gratification. He was right. He told Weirman to expect Christie and Robbins. "Peter Christie?" the professor said. "What an unfortunate name."

"What's in a name?" Morlock the warlock replied.

"About ten P.M., then. Can they find it?" Weirman asked.

"Yes. I'm sure they can."

"They must knock six times, pause, then seven more. Is the girl pretty?"

"Very."

"They are prepared for the sky-clad initiation?"

"They're looking forward to it."

"Fine, Doctor."

"Thank you, Professor."

Now Christie stood in the middle of Abigail Robbins' studio apartment and thought over the events of the past week. Absently, he helped her on with her coat.

He wasn't naked yet, but he felt close to it without his .38 Police Special. He had left it home. In its place was a thin German PPK 7.65mm automatic taped to his side under his left arm. A large square pressure bandage covered the gun. The area was smeared with iodine. A punctured boil was the story he and Ryker had decided on. Robbins wore a small .25 Beretta fastened to her head with surgical tape under a long blond wig. The three cops had realized almost too late that there weren't too many places to hide even a small gun when you were stark naked. They had come up with what they had only this morning. Unfortunately, there was no way they could hide a body-set transmitter.

Christie looked at Robbins. "Ready?"

"Ready."

They exchanged nervous jokes as they rode to the Village. Two blocks from Charles Street, they got out and began walking. They knew that at least four cops and Ryker were with them, but they saw nobody.

Christie was excited. Robbins looked composed, but was beginning to get nervous. The weather was cold and a light powdery snow began falling.

They turned onto Charles Street and walked up to the old rectory. Christie thought he heard a voice and turned sharply around.

"Keep cool or you'll have me going bananas, too," Robbins whispered.

"I'm cool."

THE HAMMER OF GOD

She took his arm and squeezed it.

They walked behind the old rectory and stopped at the bushes blocking the cellar stairs.

"Down into the fires of hell," Christie said.

"Cheer up. Morlock said the initiation wasn't so bad. It's the Grand Sabbat on April 30 I'm worried about."

"You don't mind standing there naked in front of all these people?" Christie asked.

"I'll probably freeze my tail off," she said.

They went down.

Six knocks. Pause. Seven knocks.

"Whence come you?" A heavy masculine voice came from behind the door.

Christie took a deep breath. "From the north—the place of great darkness." His voice wavered slightly.

"Wither goest thou?"

"We travel east in search of light."

"What password doth thou bring?"

"Perfect love and perfect trust."

The heavy door swung open. The young couple stepped inside. The door slammed and a bolt was thrown shut.

The challenger, a big youth in a black robe, stepped before them. He pointed a long sword at them.

"I, Guardian of the Watchtower of the North, forbid thee to enter further. Thou canst not enter this holy place from the north, save thou first be purified and consecrated. Who vouches for you?"

A girl, about fifteen, also clad in a black robe, stepped out of the darkness.

"I, Guide of Souls, so do."

The big youth lowered the sword. "Children of Darkness, approach the Watchtower of the North and receive of me the bonds of death and blessing of earth."

Christie swallowed hard as he followed the girl

through the flickering candlelight. As he approached the brick altar, he noticed a flaming brazier set in front of it. A circle of people, at least twenty, stood facing the burning altar. *At least two covens here for this,* he thought. Someone was playing a haunting tune on a reed flute. The whole effect was weird and frightening. It was meant to be.

Suddenly the young guide of souls turned, walked up to Christie, and without a word began unbuttoning his coat. A bearded youth appeared out of the darkness and did the same with Robbins. Christie stood and tried to keep his knees from shaking.

Fucking Ryker, fucking Ryker, he kept repeating to himself.

As each piece of clothing was removed, it was taken by a third person, a girl who went back and forth between the two cops as they were stripped by the guides of souls. The clothes were heaped in her arms. Christie stood in his shoes, socks, and shorts. He was cold, but he hardly noticed it; he kept glancing quickly to his right as the bearded kid stripped Robbins.

The guide knelt in front of him and grabbed his shorts by the waistband. She pulled them down and over his feet and handed them to the clothes-bearer. She removed his shoes and socks and slipped on a pair of leather sandals. She rose and smiled at him.

I want to go home, he thought.

The guide of souls eyed the bulging bandage on his left side, and Christie didn't know if he should do or say anything. He glanced at Robbins. She was naked except for her panties. The flickering candles played off her round white body. She looked unconcerned. Christie watched with mounting jealousy as the bearded kid slid her panties off and put sandals on her small feet. He knew he was in love. He felt like hammering the bearded youth into unconsciousness and dragging Abigail away from this place.

Both witches now produced a long piece of black rope. This was the part Christie, as a cop, was most concerned about. He would be helpless in a few minutes. His female guide tied his hands behind his back and passed the free end of the rope around his neck. The remainder hung down his chest. She then took a red rope and tied each ankle. The rope was long and he would be able to take near-normal strides.

Next, she held up a black blindfold. Christie looked again at Abigail Robbins. She glanced at him and winked before her blindfold covered her face. Suddenly his blindfold was on. He fought down a rising feeling of panic. If the monk came crashing through the door now, he knew he was dead. Suddenly he felt a tug on the rope around his neck; he was being led toward the circle by the guide. He cursed Ryker, Morlock, the NYPD, and Zachariah.

He was led around the outside of the great circle of witches. At each quarter circle, north, south, east, and west, he was stopped and a few words were spoken. Once, he collided with a cold, naked body; he knew it was Robbins.

He became panicky again at being blind. The chants and flute music became superaccentuated by his blindness. His female guide now put one arm around his waist and the other around his neck. The male guide did the same with Robbins. The circle opened at the northern point and the two initiates were led inside, up to the blazing altar. The naked pair felt the warmth of the fire at their backs. A female voice behind them called out, "Listen to the words of the Great Mother, who was of old called Astarte. 'At mine altars are made sacrifice. On the Great Sabbats or when the moon is full, meet in some secret place and adore me, who am queen of all magics.'"

Christie's back began to sweat. His front was cold.

He could feel many eyes staring at him; he wanted to move sideways to make contact with Robbins.

" 'There assemble,' " continued the hoarse female voice, " 'and to those who would learn sorcery, I will teach thee things unknown. And you shall be free, and as a sign that you be really so, be naked in rites, dance, sing, feast, make music and love.' "

Christie and Robbins, still clasped by their guides, were led around the interior of the circle at a fast skipping step. The flute played louder and faster; a bell began tolling as they ran. Christie felt foolish and scared at the same time. A wild idea began to take hold in his mind. He became convinced that Morlock had deceived them and that they were both going to be killed by these crazy witches. He put the idea out of his mind. It was absurd.

Suddenly, as he ran, he was drawn to an abrupt halt and led back toward the burning altar. This time he could feel Robbins' arm touching his as they stood. She rubbed her arm against his. He became excited at the small touch. Hands touched his face and the blindfold was removed. He stared at the circle of witches around him. The fire warmed his rear. Robbins slipped her foot out of her sandal and rubbed it lightly over his toes. He tensed. Hands pulled him a few feet sideways away from his companion. He wondered if he were turning red. He had never been naked in front of so large a mixed group before.

A woman, over thirty, dressed as a high priestess, walked from behind the altar and stood in front of him. A man, who he figured was Professor Weirman, came around the other side and stood in front of Abigail Robbins. The man stroked his close-cropped beard. Both cops knew that the five-fold kiss was coming; so did their audience. They tightened the circle and moved closer.

The high priestess, a striking-looking woman, knelt down in front of Christie and kissed his feet. "Blessed be thy feet that have brought thee in these ways," she intoned.

The coven responded, "Blessed be!"

She unbent a little and kissed both his knees.

"Blessed be thy knees that shall kneel at the holy altar."

"Blessed be!"

Christie tensed. The priestess's mouth was only a few inches from his penis. He tried to control the inevitable erection, but his penis stiffened and rose. It hit the bottom of her chin. She smiled slightly, and a few women who were close giggled. Christie flushed red. She drew back a bit and softly kissed the head of his erect penis. "Blessed be thy organ of generation, without which we would not be," she said. Her warm breath blew against his excited organ. Vapor came from her mouth in the cold room.

"Blessed be!" the assembled witches said loudly.

The high priestess rose and grabbed him by the arms. His outthrust penis touched her belly. He thought he might come if he lost control. She bent over and kissed each of his breasts. "Blessed be thy breasts, formed in beauty and in strength."

She straightened up and pressed her full warm mouth over his. She held the kiss perhaps a second longer than the ceremony required. There was some tittering from the crowd. She drew back and looked into his eyes. She was dark and very pretty. She moved her belly slightly against his penis. His muscles tensed. Christie was falling in love again.

"Blessed be thy lips that shall utter the sacred words."

"Blessed be," sighed the circle.

Christie was trembling. Against his better judgment, he turned his head and looked at Abigail Robbins. She was staring straight ahead. He wondered if she had been watching.

The high priest, Weirman, knelt before Robbins, who was shaking slightly now. Christie wondered if it was the cold or the excitement. Jealousy flooded over him again.

The high priest knelt and kissed Robbins' feet. He spoke the blessing and unbent; the crowd made the response. He kissed each shaking knee slowly. As he did, he grasped each of Robbins' calves as though to steady her shaking legs. Christie was furious, but the worst was yet to come. After the intonation, the professor unbent and sunk his bearded face between Robbins' thighs. He grasped her firm buttocks with his hairy hands and Christie's erection rose still higher in spite of himself. He knew he shouldn't be watching, but he couldn't turn away. As the bearded high priest lingered a moment between Abigail Robbins' thighs, she flushed red and moved her pelvis. Weirman squeezed her buttocks and said the blessing.

He stood and grasped her arms. Slowly and smoothly, he planted a wet kiss on each of her nipples. The nipples stood out, erect and hard. He blessed her breasts.

Then he took Abigail Robbins' face in his hands and kissed her passionately. The crowd stirred again. The high priest stepped back and looked her up and down. She quivered.

The priest and priestess then grabbed their respective charges by the ropes around their necks and turned them to face the burning altar. The ropes were pulled down, forcing each of them to crouch. Both ropes were tied to a ring set in the stone floor. Christie felt Robbins quivering as their arms and legs met.

The priest and priestess then asked each in turn if they would be true to the Goddess Astarte. As they answered affirmatively a bell tolled. After a few more questions, a boy and girl appeared with long birch sticks tied with black bows.

Christie felt the first blow land on his rump. It was a light blow but it stung. Robbins gave a small cry, more of surprise than of pain as the birch switch hit her backside. The blows rained down very lightly, but there were forty of them and the cumulative effect was painful.

The initiates were untied from the ring and stood again. The high priest and priestess anointed their breasts and genitals with oil, then wine, then another kiss. Christie's erection, which had never completely died, returned in full strength. He had watched as Professor Weirman dipped his fingers into a bowl of oil, then thrust them between Robbins' legs. Christie's initiator lingered over his penis as she rubbed in the oil and wine. Morlock had assured them that these would be only ceremonial kisses and touches and that they would last but a fraction of a second. Apparently he didn't realize that the priest and priestess would be so attracted to their charges.

Finally, the initiates' hands and feet were unbound and a ring with a witch's mark was presented to each of them. A large book was brought before them and they each signed their witch's name in runic letters. Christie had chosen Balaam; Robbins, Brisen.

The couple was paraded naked around the circle again, while each witch and warlock embraced them and kissed them. Christie didn't mind the girls, but he winced when the men kissed him on the lips. By this time, however, he was numb from the cold and at least each embrace was warming to his frigid body. He completed the circle and stood looking at Robbins. She was taking much longer. Jealously, he wondered if it were because she was being held longer or if she was purposely lingering over the kisses. She held the female kisses just as long as the male ones, Christie noticed; he was seething inside.

At last they were led to a dark corner where their clothes were waiting. They dressed silently in the dark. The challenger approached them with the sword; Christie faced him.

"Go now out," the challenger said loudly. "Thou art witch, and thou art warlock. Be true to our faith. Come ye back at the next Esbat one week hence." He turned and walked off. The pair of newborn witches finished dressing and slipped out the door into the cold night. Morlock had told them that they probably wouldn't be asked to stay for the remainder of the Esbat. The witches would want to discuss their new converts.

As they walked silently out to the street, Robbins said, "They had about two covens there, I guess."

"Yeah."

They walked. *Where the hell is Ryker,* Christie thought. He stopped and faced Robbins; neither spoke or looked into the other's eyes. Christie turned away and began walking again.

"You seemed to enjoy yourself," he said softly, an edge in his voice.

"I knew that was coming," she said.

"Did you?"

"Yes." She paused. "I seem to remember *your* flag flying at full mast, if I'm not mistaken."

"What the hell did you expect me—"

"What the hell did you expect from me? I'm human, you know."

"So you enjoyed it, then?"

"That's right," she snapped. "So much so that I'm going to join every coven in town just so I can get my twat kissed."

"Shut up."

They walked in silence.

Ryker pulled up in an unmarked car. The two cops got in. Ryker knew there'd be a scene between the two of them, if he had judged his two young partners correctly. He said nothing during the trip uptown. A few minutes later they pulled up in front of Christie's building.

"Full report at the station house at eight sharp," Ryker said.

Christie nodded wordlessly, got out, and slammed the door.

Ryker shook his head and drove the car around the corner to Abigail Robbins' apartment.

"I'd invite you up, but I'm kind of tired," Robbins said.

"I'd accept, but I'm sure you're all fucked out," Ryker said.

"Bastard. Can't you ever be serious?"

"I am. All the time," Ryker said.

FOURTEEN

For the next few weeks, Ryker settled into a more normal caseload, working on small-time, PDU-handled murders of junkies and prostitutes. He never asked much about Christie's weekly Esbats, and Christie didn't offer much information. Ryker suspected that his young partner was lovesick, and Ryker had no time for love.

Spring came at last to the frozen city. The detectives never got back to Zachariah's lair. They had two leads, however. A liquor dealer on Bowery told a team of detectives that a huge monk had come in about four months before and purchased four cases of Riunite wine. The big man refused an offer to deliver the cases and picked them all up at one time and carried them off. A cheese dealer nearby had a similar story.

Zachariah fasted and prayed for days on end as he steeled himself for the upcoming Sabbat of Walpurgis Night. He never left his room except to empty his chamber pot in the small hours of the morning.

He managed to suppress feelings of worthlessness at his inaction by reminding himself that on the witches'

Grand Sabbat, he would double his efforts to save as many from evil as possible. Zachariah also placed a faded photo of his mother by the large white candle. He liked to look at her while he scourged himself with a knotted whip. The fresh blood flowing down his back cleansed his soul.

Lindly began coordinating the surveillance at various theaters around town for Walpurgis Night.

Christie and Robbins went to their Friday-night Esbats, barely on speaking terms. They arrived separately and left separately, while a four- or six-person team flitted around the Charles Street rectory like phantoms each Friday night. Ryker was usually with them. Zachariah never came.

During an Esbat a few weeks before Walpurgis Night, Julia Preston returned to her coven. She was shaky and sad, but she had lost weight during her convalescence and looked prettier than before her ordeal. Christie held his breath as he waited to see if she would recognize him from the hospital. When he and Robbins were introduced to her as new members, she just smiled at him in the dim candlelight. He sighed with relief. Ryker had been right as usual. She wouldn't have remembered her own mother from the hospital.

With the death of her roommate and lover, Wendy Willo, Julia Preston had returned to the coven looking for strength and companionship. She managed to sit close to Christie whenever possible.

The weekly Esbats were remarkably mild for a witches' coven. Mostly the young people sat around and talked about psychic experiences or discussed magic spells and potions. Lectures on witchcraft were given by Professor Weirman, who managed to leave with a different girl each Friday night, presumably to explore with her the deeper meaning of the ancient art. Each week he asked Abbie Robbins to accompany him home. Every week she refused. But Weirman was patient. He intended to have her at the Grand Sabbat when no request could be refused. The high priestess, Sarah Coventry, who was a switch-hitter, had also asked Abbie Robbins to come home with her, but was politely refused.

Zachariah broke his fast on the Monday before Walpurgis Night. At two A.M., he slipped quietly into the communal bathroom near his room, he emptied his chamber pot, and gathered up all the loose magazines and newspapers which lay scattered about. He returned to his solitary room and lit the huge white candle on the floor. Ever since the day the police had come, he had been burning with anxiety. *Had they been looking for him?* He felt positive they were. The agents of Lucifer were closing in.

He scanned the several papers, but could find no references to himself. As he turned over the wrinkled pages in the flickering light, his coal-black eyes caught something odd. He looked closer. At the bottom of the entertainment page in the *Daily News* was a small black-bordered box, a column wide and three inches high. Inside the box was a witch's wheel. He stared, fascinated. He peered closer at the runic lettering. Abruptly, he threw aside the paper and dove onto the floor, rummaged through the things under his bed, and came up with a black-bound book, *The Secrets of the Black Arts.* He tore through the yellowed pages until he found the key to the runic alphabet. Then, kneeling over the bed, he began translating furiously. He wrote in the margin of the newspaper as he worked.

After a few minutes, he had the addresses of the two coven meetings. He stared hard at one of them.

"Charles Street. The rectory basement," it said. "Weekly Esbats."

He put his trembling hands over his sweating face. He felt God had sent him this message as a reward for his devotion.

He knew vaguely where East 65th Street was, but he wondered about Charles Street; he wondered if he could bring the wrath of God down on both unholy houses on the same Sabbat night. If he had to choose one or the other, he would choose the church rectory. He was outraged at the blasphemy of using a hallowed place for so unholy a purpose.

He tore through the other papers. More black-bordered boxes. The messages were the same. He thought about striking the Charles Street coven on the upcoming Esbat, Friday, and then the East 65th Street coven on Walpurgis Night, Monday. He struggled with his dilemma. At length, he knelt on the side of his bed and prayed for guidance. He prayed until dawn.

As the sun broke through the window, Zachariah fell to the floor and slept. God had told him what to do.

The Friday before the Grand Sabbat on April 30, two new witches, a man and a woman, were initiated. Christie and Robbins watched as the embarrassed couple went through the sky-clad ceremony. Christie wondered if he and Abbie looked as silly and as frightened when they stood naked at the altar. He glanced toward his partner. She was looking at him. She smiled. He turned away.

After the meeting, she followed him out.

"Balaam," she called, using his witch's name with a smile.

He turned. "What?"

"Walk with me."

They walked in silence.

"Monday is Walpurgis Night, Balaam."

"Don't use that stupid name."

"Why not? It sounds nice. It's better than Christie for a warlock."

"I'm not a warlock or a witch. I'm Peter Christie."

"I'm Brisen, the wicked witch of East 55th Street," she said, laughing.

"I think you're taking this a little too seriously. You're really enjoying this shit, aren't you?"

She hesitated. "Well, they're different. Our initiation ceremony left a deep impression on me. I felt funny afterwards."

"I'm sure you did," he said.

"Come on, Christie, call me a whore and get it over with," she said calmly.

"You know, you should have been more professional about that initiation. You should have been more aloof—more detached. You let it get the better of you. You're letting these meetings go to your head. We're here as undercover cops, not witches."

"Look who's talking about professionalism," she said. "Your dick was sticking into the high priestess's belly as I recall."

So you were watching, he thought.

"Besides that," she continued, "you've been ogling Julia Preston for the last month. That part of the case is over. We don't need her anymore."

They stood on the corner, waiting for Ryker. Abigail Robbins was upset.

"What's the matter?" Christie asked.

"Nothing."

"Tell me."

She looked up at him. "Next week. I'm frightened. The Black Mass. The orgy. Zachariah. Will you stay close to me?" she covered her face with her hand.

Christie didn't know what to do. Finally, he put his arm around her shoulders.

"You're not going. Don't worry."

She looked up with a start. "What?"

"You're not going. Ryker and I discussed it. We decided it wasn't necessary. I was going to tell you."

"Why?"

"It's just not necessary, damn it."

"I want to go. It's my job."

"I don't need you. If Zachariah doesn't show, all you'll get is screwed. It's not worth it."

"And if he doesn't show I have to attend meetings until the next Sabbat. How will it look if I don't show for this one? A Sabbat is important."

"This was your last meeting, period. I'll attend them all from here on in—if there are any more after Monday. You're off the case."

"What if he does show up?" She was angry. "Do you think you can handle him all by yourself, smart-ass?"

"He'll never get past the surveillance team anyway. Forget it. Drop it. You're off the case. You did a fine job for us. Thank you."

"Us? Who the hell do you think you are? You're just a fucking silver shield. You can't order me around, Christie."

"Balaam." He smiled.

She wasn't smiling. "Listen, this is my case, too. I don't need a bunch of assholes like you to make things easy for me."

"Wait. Wait. A minute ago you were scared stiff."

"So what! Part of being a cop is being scared."

"Okay, okay. Let's talk about it someplace else."

She suddenly seemed pacified. "My place or yours?"

She took his arm as an unmarked car pulled up next to them.

They slept at her place that night.

On Monday, April 30, the Grand Sabbat of Walpurgis Night, Joe Ryker checked his .357 Magnum and his .38 Police Special. He paced like a caged tiger up and down the length of the long conference room. The grimy, round wall clock said 7:40 P.M.

The task force, which had been mired in its own inertia, was suddenly full of bustle and purpose. Deputy Inspector Connolly had managed to steal a full complement of troops to cover the theaters, Morlock's apartment, and the Charles Street rectory. But all the detectives present at the newly invigorated command center knew that this was the last shot they'd have at the monk. If he didn't show up tonight, they'd all have new jobs in the morning. Several new murders a day were taking precedence and the public had long since forgotten the butchered "witches."

"Why the fuck doesn't Lindly call?" Ryker said to no one in particular.

"It's not eight yet. None of the productions starts before seven-thirty," Connolly said. "You think he'll show?"

"How the fuck do I know?" Ryker said irritably. "You worried about your job?"

"Enough, Ryker," Connolly said, reaching into the pocket of his cream-colored suit coat for his tranquilizers. He *did* want to nail the monk, if only to prove to his bosses that he was still capable of doing good police work. But to make the bust, he had had to make two important decisions, decisions he wondered if he'd regret later. First, he had shown to the P.C.—personally—that he needed the vast manpower to snatch the monk. If the son of a bitch didn't show, he,

Connolly, would be retired early or sent back to the Twinky Hilton on Long Island.

He gulped three more tranquilizers, wondering if he could close his eyes and wish it all away. He had thought about that often, as if by an act of will he could simply make it all disappear. He had read a short story once about a man who claimed that if he went to sleep, the earth and all the people on it would disappear, for he had created everything in his mind. Everyone thought the man was crazy. But when the poor bastard dozed off, sure enough, everything disappeared.

Connolly opened his eyes, but all he saw was Ryker's hard face staring at him with total contempt.

That was his second regrettable decision, he thought, trying to look Ryker in the eye: putting Ryker in charge. The sergeant was too direct, too violent, a relic from another age. He didn't have the suave, intellectual approach to police work that the politicians demanded these days.

Connolly shuddered, turning away from Ryker's icy green eyes—snake eyes. He never should have allowed Ryker to infiltrate those two cops into the coven. If one of them got hurt or the newspapers discovered they'd been fucking their brains out for the Big Blue Machine, they'd all be parking-lot attendants at the police pound.

Suddenly, three phones rang almost simultaneously. Ryker, Lieutenant Fischetti, and Wilkinson each grabbed one, exchanged a few short words with the detectives calling, and hung up. The phones rang again. More detectives were reporting in from all the theaters where Zachariah might strike. By eight-thirty, the crowds, such as they were on a Monday night, had filled the theaters. No monk. No one in regular clothes matching his description. Lindly finally called from Lincoln Center. Ryker took it.

"Well?" He could hear a lot of people in the background.

The voice was edgy, worried. "Big crowd here for a Monday."

"I don't give a shit. This motherfucker is seven feet tall. Is he there?"

"No."

Ryker exhaled slowly. "Did you check his seat?"

"Empty."

"I think you should stay there. Sit in his seat. Maybe he'll show up later and sit in your lap. If he doesn't, enjoy the show."

"Sure. Anything from anyone else?"

"No."

"I think that ad pulled him away, Joe. I think he'll be at East 65th Street or Charles Street tonight."

"Could be. Everyone will stay put, though."

"Right. When are you going to East 65th Street?"

"Morlock's expecting me about 11:30, so I'll probably go now."

"Be careful."

Ryker hung up. Connolly looked worried as he turned to Ryker. "No luck?"

"Not yet," Ryker said, lighting a cigar.

"We'll know in a few hours, I suppose," Connolly said vaguely. His head felt heavy. Like he wanted to drift off to sleep. Perhaps when he woke up, everything would be all right.

"What the fuck's wrong with you?" Ryker said, staring at his commander. "You're supposed to be running this show and you're higher than a fucking junkie. Wake up!"

Startled, Connolly opened his eyes and looked around. The conference room was absolutely still. Everyone was looking at him; he hadn't the slightest clue who they were or what they wanted. He smiled and said, "Hello."

"Shit," Fischetti said, coming to Connolly's aid. "Help me get him out of here."

Ryker laughed. "Asshole," he said. "Give my regards to the Zoogs."

"Zoogs?" Connolly said. "Why, of course."

By nine o'clock Connolly was safely strapped into the nutmobile on the way back out to Long Island and Ryker was in charge until Lieutenant Fischetti showed he had some balls. It would be a long wait.

"Sometimes it's difficult to tell the nuts from the bolts," Ryker said, lighting another cigar. "Where the fuck is Christie?"

"On his way, I guess," Wilkinson said.

Ryker walked over to his desk and retrieved a flask of bourbon. He took a long pull.

At 9:15 Christie walked in, looking nervous and a little pale. "Anything from the theaters?"

"No. You're going to the Sabbat, Balaam."

"Great. Just fucking great."

"We have patrols all around. If we spot him on the street, we'll grab him or follow him. We'll make that decision on the spot."

"Good idea," Christie said, sitting in a swivel chair.

"I'm full of good ideas," Ryker said. "Listen, kid, we can't get word to you once you're in that basement, so call right before you enter and get a status report."

"Right. Listen, as long as you're full of good ideas, did you come up with something for my gun? I don't want to go in there armed with nothing except my hard dick. I don't think we can get away with that bandage routine again. I'll be bare-assed naked with a lot of hands all over me." Christie looked worried.

Ryker opened his desk drawer and pulled out a leather bag hanging from a rawhide thong. He held it up. "Morlock came up with this. It's a witch's amulet. You wear it around your neck."

Christie stood up and looked at it. "You going to join Connolly or something? I'll need more than a fucking magic charm if Zachariah tries to chop my head off."

"There's a .25 Beretta automatic in it, asshole. One magazine, seven rounds. I hope you won't need it, but keep it close." Ryker threw it to him. "Morlock said it won't look out of place even if you're bare-assed."

Christie examined it. "Oh. Okay. Good." There were runic letters burned into the stiff leather. In addition to the gun, the bag was stuffed with a sweet-smelling herb. Small snaps made for a quick opening, but he wasn't completely satisfied. "You couldn't ram a bigger caliber in there?"

Ryker frowned. "We tried, but we couldn't make the bag any bigger without it looking out of place. There's enough punch there if you use it right."

"Okay. I won't be needing it anyway."

"That's a bad attitude to take with a gun. If you don't have confidence in it we can—"

"No, no. It's okay. It's too late anyway."

"Okay," Ryker said to Wilkinson. "I'm going to Morlock's before his company arrives. If by some chance we nail the monk before then, call me there. Christie, stay here until the last possible minute, then split for Charles Street."

"Right."

Ryker took his trenchcoat and walked toward the stairs. He turned around. "Where's Robbins?"

"Home. I just left her."

"Was she pissed?"

"Yeah."

"Good hunting."

"Thanks."

Ryker walked outside and got into a battered Plymouth. The night was warm and mild. He gave the driver Abigail Robbins' address. There was no doubt in his mind that she would be at the Sabbat on Charles Street against orders. Christie didn't seem to know this. Short of throwing her in the squad lockup for the night, there was no way to keep her away and Ryker knew it. When the car stopped at her apartment, he got out and walked into the lobby. He approached the elderly doorman and showed his badge.

"Abigail Robbins in?"

"I'll check, sir."

"Just see if she's in, that's all."

The doorman rang her apartment. She answered and he pretended he'd rung the wrong apartment, apologized, and hung up.

Ryker handed him a brown paper parcel. "See that she gets this if she leaves tonight." He slipped the doorman a five.

"Yes, sir."

Ryker got back into the car and arrived at Morlock's ten minutes later. Detective Fernandez was dressed in the French field marshal uniform of the apartment house doorman. Ryker smiled as Fernandez touched his patent-leather cap visor.

"You look good, Fernandez. Maybe you should consider this full time."

"Maybe. I made twenty bucks in tips already."

Ryker flipped him a dime and walked into the huge lobby. Detective Ward, dressed in coveralls, was pushing a large dust broom across the black marble floor.

"You missed a spot near that armchair."

"Take it up with my union."

Ryker entered the elevator and got off at the thirteenth floor. Morlock answered the door himself.

"You're early," Morlock said.

"Yeah? I like it better when the butler answers the door, by the way." He walked in.

"Did you catch him yet?"

"I wouldn't be here if we did, would I?" He began

walking down the hall. Suddenly, he stopped. "Where's the door to the hidden room?"

Morlock stared for a moment, then walked over to a spot on the paneled wall and pushed. The panel swung slowly inward. Ryker followed Morlock into the dark room. The doctor turned on a small lamp. The cop looked around. The room was filled with folding tables and chairs. Black robes hung from the walls and all types of paraphernalia for a Sabbat were strewn over the floor. Animal masks were hanging on a far wall.

"Witches' warehouse, huh, Doc?"

"I suppose that's what you'd call it. It's also the dressing room. You can get undressed here now. Find a robe that fits. There are clothes trees scattered about." He waved his hand. "Nothing on under the robe and no shoes, please."

"Can I wear my badge?"

"No. Will you be wearing your gun?"

"Is the pope Catholic?"

"I couldn't care less what he is," Morlock said. "What will you do when everyone, uh, disrobes? I don't want you frightening my guests."

"I didn't think witches frightened so easily." Ryker sat down on a folding chair. "I'll slip my gun and holster under the couch when the action starts. Unless of course someone wants to suck on my gun muzzle."

"I hardly think so."

"I don't think I'll need it anyway, Doc, so relax."

"I should hope you won't. I agree with you, by the way. I think if he saw our advertisement, he will go to the church rectory on Charles Street."

"Probably."

"Well, why do you want to stay here, then? Maybe you should be there to help your—"

"Hey, Doc. I'm in charge here, remember?"

Morlock turned and left the hidden room, the color rising in his pale cheeks. Ryker stripped and strapped on his shoulder holster with his .357 Magnum. He slipped on a black robe and chose a lion's mask from the wall. He felt foolish as he walked back into the long hall and into the large bloodred chamber.

The room was lit with dozens of long black candles set in silver candelabras. In the corner by the fireplace was a rolling bar. Ryker walked over and poured himself a drink. He set his lion's mask on the mantel and lit a cigar. Morlock walked by several times but ignored him. He stood and watched as three men, dressed in conventional busboy clothing, began removing the witches' paraphernalia from the hidden room and setting it up in the large chamber. A sort of portable horned altar was placed in the middle of the room. Ryker sat in an armchair and watched as the room was slowly transformed into a witches' playground.

By 10:30 P.M., the witches and warlocks began arriving individually and in groups. They all changed into robes and masked themselves in the hidden room, then entered the large chamber. Ryker slipped on his lion's mask and found that he could still sip bourbon and smoke a cigar through the mouth opening. He wondered how stupid he looked. Other witches were wearing the faces of bats, cats, panthers, wolves, and other predatory animals. They moved around like phantoms in the candlelit room. A few of them tried to make conversation with Ryker, but he kept blowing cigar smoke in their faces and they eventually moved off.

Ryker was waiting for the phone to ring. He was waiting for Wilkinson to tell him that they had grabbed Zachariah.

Finally, it rang at 11:10, and the butler managed to

get his attention from across the crowded room. With a mixture of relief and disappointment, he found a quiet corner and picked up the receiver.

"Ryker," he said, but his voice was muffled by the lion's head and he realized he couldn't hear a damned thing. Turning his back on the early arrivals, he slipped the mask off and said, "Where'd they grab him?"

"Grab who?"

"Who is this?"

"It's Ellie. What's wrong, Joe?"

"My God," Ryker said. "How did you get this number?"

"Lieutenant Fischetti gave it to me. He was sorry about my pet pig or something. What did he mean by that?" Ellie said. "Those guys you work with are pretty strange."

"Look, Ellie, I really can't talk right now. I'm at an orgy."

"Sure, Joe. Don't kid me. You're probably busy on a case or something." She was laughing. In spite of everything, that made Ryker feel better. "No, really, Ellie. I'm at an orgy with a bunch of witches."

"It's okay," Ellie said. "I just called to say hello. I know when I'm bothering you, so I'll hang up. An orgy, really." She was laughing again.

"It's true," he said. "I could use some of those underpants you're hawking right about now. I'm not wearing anything but a robe and a lion's mask."

She laughed even harder, gasping for breath. "A lion's mask? Come on, Joe, I can't stand anymore. I'll talk to you later, when you've sobered up. That's the funniest thing I ever heard. Forget what I said about you not having a sense of humor. Witches! See you, Joe."

"Hold it," he said. "Just one more thing."

"I know, you turn into a killer tomato at midnight."

"No, seriously. I just wanted to say . . . I'm glad you called."

"So am I," she said. "Wait until I tell Sidney about the lion's mask. Bye, Joe."

Ryker put the receiver carefully back in the cradle. He had almost said that he loved her. But that was the trouble with Ellie, she and reality seemed as incompatible as . . . husband and wife.

By 11:20, forty people were milling around the room. Most of them looked elderly even through their disguises. Ryker noticed that most of them walked rich. They had an air of money and decadence about them. Several young people, male and female prostitutes, arrived in a single group escorted by a warlock. They were all stripped in the hidden room and led into the big chamber. They sat around naked, smoking hashish, marijuana, and crack, and snorting coke.

Ryker walked over to Morlock.

"Is everyone here?"

"It seems so."

"What time does this thing start?"

"Midnight, of course. We begin with a rather mild version of the Black Mass—not like the one your friends will be experiencing in about an hour. Then comes the feast followed by the, uh, orgy."

"Do you play spin the bottle?"

"Post office," Morlock said in a rare display of humor.

Ryker walked toward the hallway. It was 11:30. He never really thought the monk would show up here. If he had planned to hit both places in one night, he would probably have been here already and hit the downtown address second. Ryker slid through the swinging panel door and into the dark room. A huge attendant was standing in the room. Ryker hadn't anticipated this. He called the man over. The big man stood fast.

"Who are you? The hat-check girl?"

No answer.

Ryker didn't feel like wasting time with this guy. He reached under his robe and pulled out his big Magnum.

"Turn around, motherfucker."

The big man looked at the gun and turned slowly around. Ryker brought the butt of the Magnum down with everything he had. The man stood for a second before his knees buckled.

Quickly but methodically, Ryker went through all the jacket pockets, pants pockets, and purses. In ten minutes he had about forty different pieces of identification. He didn't know it at the time, but he had in his hand the names of two state senators, a congresswoman, three judges, plus a host of prominent bankers, businessmen, and professional people. In addition, he had the badge of a deputy police commissioner, obviously Morlock's inside source of information. To Ryker it was like rubbing a magic lamp and getting forty wishes. It was like forty scissors cutting through miles of red tape at some future date.

Quickly, because time was running out, he slipped into the hall and out the door, still robed and barefoot. In three minutes he was outside on the sidewalk. The unmarked car had no trouble spotting him and pulled alongside the curb. Ryker jumped in.

"Let's go!"

Procino made a U-turn on the wide avenue and swung south.

"Anything from Charles Street yet?"

"Nothing." The cop slapped a portable dome light on the roof and hit the switches. The red light spun and the siren wailed. Ryker dropped his bundle of loot plus his own wallet on the seat.

"Guard this stuff with your life, Procino."

The car started gathering speed. With any luck Ryker would be on Charles Street in time. He looked at his watch. Midnight. The Grand Sabbat of Walpurgis Night had begun.

FIFTEEN

Christie had hung around the station house until 10:30 waiting for a break, but Zachariah was still loose.

A little after 11 P.M., he entered the basement of the Charles Street rectory. He hadn't spotted any cops on the way in, but he knew that at least eight of them were there.

Inside, near the door, he passed the challenger and removed his clothes. He laid them on a long table already strewn with both men's and women's clothing and picked out a black robe made of dyed bedsheets; he slipped his feet into a pair of worn sandals. Before he pulled on the tattered robe, Julia Preston approached him. She was already dressed in a short, tight-fitting robe. She greeted him with a smile and fingered the leather amulet on his bare chest. Christie took a small step back.

"It smells like balm of Gilead and frankincense," she said and smiled.

"It's cheese dip for later."

ʹ Julia laughed and ran her hands over his naked chest. She touched the amulet again.

"There's something hard in there."

"It's a gun." He smiled.

"Why aren't you ever serious, Peter?" She looked him up and down. "Last night I dreamt that I was in the hospital and you came to see me."

"Were you having a baby?"

Julia laughed again and watched as Christie pulled on the not-too-clean robe. He rummaged through some cheap Halloween masks on the table and picked out a monkey face and put it on. Julia hid her face in her hands as she tried to control her laughter.

"What's so funny?"

She shook her head, threw her own mask on the table and found another monkey mask. She slipped it on and they both walked together toward the altar.

Christie noticed that the floor was strewn with musty old mattresses, pillows, air mattresses, and old blankets. He and the girl knelt on pillows arranged in a circle and faced the burning altar. About a dozen other robed and masked witches had already arrived and were also kneeling in the circle.

Christie looked up at the altar. Plaster statues of saints were lined up on the altar, between the two burning black candles. Each of the statues had been desecrated in some way. Colored wax had been used to add penises to the male statues and large bare breasts to the female ones. Some of the statues had wax horns. A large alabaster female nude sat on the floor at the base of the altar. The original head had been removed and in its place, the head of Christ was stuck on with plaster. A statue of a horse held the head of Mary. In addition, a large wooden cross hung upside down from the ceiling by a chain.

Christie felt slightly nauseated. He rocked back on his haunches. The sweet smell of the amulet, added to musky odors from the basement, made his stomach churn. He fought down the sickness and looked around the circle. More people had arrived; at least twenty masked and robed witches and warlocks knelt and chanted. There were pillows for at least twenty more. People arrived every few minutes, stripped, slipped on a robe and mask, and knelt in the circle.

Julia Preston reached out and took Christie's hand. At the same time, the girl on his opposite side tapped him on the shoulder. He turned his head and was presented with a hashish pipe. He took a small toke and passed it to Julia Preston. She inhaled long and slowly and passed it on. *Powerful shit,* he thought.

The pipe kept getting refilled and passed around. Christie tried to inhale as little as possible, but he had a slight buzz on nonetheless. He felt his senses were getting clouded and his reaction time was slowing. He knew it for sure when he looked up and saw Abigail Robbins kneeling in the circle less than fifteen feet from him, close to the altar. She was wearing a fox mask, but he would know her no matter what she was wearing. He raised his mask, stared, and blinked. She raised her own mask, winked back, and smiled. Around her neck hung a leather amulet. He couldn't see it well in the half-light, but he knew it was the mate to his own.

"Motherfucking Ryker," he said.

"Ryker?" Preston whispered. "Don't blaspheme, Peter."

"The motherfucking Devil."

"That's better. A new name for him. Lucifer, Satan, Mephistopheles, the Horned One, the Lord of Misrule, and Motherfucking Devil." She giggled.

Christie was going to walk over and drag Robbins out by the scruff of her neck, but as he began to get up, Preston and the girl on the other side of him each

206

grabbed his robe and pulled him down. A bell began ringing in the darkness.

From behind the altar, he could see two figures coming toward him. They seemed to rise in the air as they grew nearer to the burning altar. They were both stark naked except that the man wore a full goat's head and the woman the head of a black cat. Christie blinked and rubbed his eyes. The figures rose higher. He realized that they must be walking up a ramp at the rear of the altar.

They stood now on the top of the ramp, behind and above the altar, the fire, and the desecrated statues.

Christie knew that the two figures must be Weirman and his high priestess, Sarah Coventry, but they seemed larger than life, huge creatures of evil. The Sabbat had begun. Christie looked at his watch. Twenty minutes to twelve. Someone had jumped the gun a bit.

"Greetings!" the goat called out and threw up his hands. "Hail, Children of Darkness!"

"Hail, Great Horned One!" the assembly answered.

"Tonight, the Holy Night of Walpurgis, the spirits fly and the demons howl and the smell of death rides upon the air. The very earth opens and the gates of hell send forth our lord and master—Satan!"

"Hail Satan! Blessed be!"

Christie felt a chill run down his spine. A flute began playing somewhere in the darkness; the circle rose in unison. They all turned left, including Christie, and began walking single file around to the back of the altar.

Christie had only a vague idea of what was going on. Morlock had said that each coven celebrated the Grand Sabbat in a slightly different manner, but there were some common practices. One of these was the *osculam obscoenum* or obscene kiss, which was what was taking place now, Christie noticed. Each witch and warlock filed up the ramp where the goat-man was bent over with his bare buttocks facing the approaching children of darkness. Each witch knelt, raised his mask and payed homage to the Devil by kissing the goat-man's anus. They then filed down the ramp and resumed their positions in the circle around the altar. The cat-woman watched silently with her arms folded over her bare breasts as the procession filed by. Christie turned away as Abigail Robbins, about a dozen people in front of him, knelt and kissed the upturned anus. He closed his eyes and winced as he performed the *osculam obscoenum*.

Christie had to rate that as one of the most disagreeable experiences in his life. He had heard of kissing ass to get ahead in an organization, he told himself, but making a public religious ceremony of it was something else. As he passed behind Abbie Robbins on the way back to his place in the circle, he pulled her hair.

The musty odor of the basement was becoming overwhelmed by the smell of burning hashish, marijuana, and crack. Christie kept himself as straight as he could, but people around him, including Julia Preston, were becoming very high. The flute played and the witches chanted ancient Celtic songs. Someone began playing a fast staccato beat on a drum. The high priest and priestess continued standing with arms folded at the top of the ramp behind the altar. Their full head masks looked frightening in the flickering light.

The witches began to grow restless. They chanted, screamed, cackled, clapped and howled. A few of them ran up to the altar and heaped obscenities on the desecrated Christian statues. A warlock, partly dressed as a priest with a Roman collar, moved up to the altar and began the Black Mass. He bellowed like a steer, raised his robe, and did an obscene dance in front of the statues and ended by urinating on them. Several of the witches broke away from the frenzied circle and also urinated on the desecrated statues.

Every obscenity and blasphemy Christie had ever heard was heaped on these symbols of Christianity. A young girl lay down in front of the altar, pulled up her robe, and began masturbating with a statue of Paul. Obscene act followed obscene act. Christie had never seen such mocking and ridicule. His head swam as he stood and watched. The flute played louder and the drums beat faster. Everyone was on his feet now screaming obscenities at God and the church.

Some of the witches began chanting for Satan to come up from hell and show himself to his children. The witches were clearly working themselves into a frenzy for the orgy which followed the Black Mass. The mock priest was concluding the Black Mass with a contemptuous burlesque of the Sacrament of Communion. He had lifted his robes and was pouring wine over his genitals. Several of the witches formed a line and kneeled. The bogus priest moved sideways down the line as everyone sucked the wine from his genitals. He was cackling, "This is my body and my blood. Come eat. Come drink."

Christie moved slowly away from Julia Preston and made his way toward his partner. He came up behind her, took her by the arm and moved her into the shadows. She was trembling as she held on to him.

"Oh, God, Peter. Have you ever seen . . ."

"Don't think about it." He put his arm around her shaking shoulders.

Almost against their will, they stared back into the pool of light around the altar. The Sabbat went on, becoming more and more lewd and abandoned. Some of the witches had already ripped off their robes and were having intercourse around the altar. Christie could see lesbian and homosexual couplings also. Robbins squeezed his arm.

"I can't believe these are the same people we met at the weekly Esbats," she said quietly.

"They're nuts," Christie agreed, then added, "What the hell are you doing here?"

"I couldn't let you come alone. Do you think the monk will come?"

"If he does, he'll be real pissed off when he sees *this.*" He looked back at the reckless scene around the altar. "Well, in a way it's not as bad as I'd thought. All this blasphemy seems pretty much voluntary except for that ass-kissing. If I had to do any of that—" He stopped in midsentence. The high priest with the goat's head was pointing at them from his perch above the altar. "Oh, shit. We'd better get back to the party."

They reentered the circle of light. Christie pulled his partner down onto an old mattress. They both ripped off their robes and masks. Christie lay on top of Abbie Robbins as much to protect her as to make love to her. A lesbian couple rolled around on a blanket next to the two cops. One of the girls was tickling Christie's side with her toes. The whole floor was now covered with a sea of twisting, writhing flesh. Masks and robes were strewn around among the frolicking, squirming bodies. The drums and flute continued to play amidst the squeals and laughing of uninhibited sex. The goat-man and cat-woman continued to survey their disciples with folded arms. The goat-man had an erect penis.

A young man suddenly threw himself on Christie's back as Christie moved gently up and down in Abbie Robbins. The couple had the wind knocked out of them. The man was trying furiously to penetrate Christie's anus, but the cop had tensed the muscles of his buttocks. Hastily, he rolled over and quickly delivered a short powerful chop to the man's neck with the knife edge of his hand. The man went loose and lay limp over Christie's naked body. The cop looked around quickly. No one had seemed to notice.

Robbins extricated herself from under the two men. She said to Christie, "I think my deodorant just quit." She crawled a few feet away on her hands and knees and was immediately grabbed by a man and woman. The man held her legs up and open while the woman buried her face in Robbins' thighs, licking furiously at her vagina. Robbins didn't know if she should struggle or submit, so she stayed motionless as her face flushed red.

Christie was on his hands and knees also, crawling toward his partner. Suddenly a woman slid under his body like a mechanic under a car. Christie unexpectedly found that his penis was in her mouth. Abruptly, the woman raised her legs and hooked them around his head. She pulled until he found his face buried between her sweating thighs. The pungent female smell filled his nostrils. Even in the half-light he could see globs of white semen left by her previous lover between the lips. He was more than a little excited as the girl's mouth swallowed and reswallowed his erect penis, again and again. She tugged insistently down on his head with her smooth legs. Half-laughing and half-panicky, he remembered what Ryker had told him weeks before: "No muff-diving at this orgy, Christie. That's the surest way of being caught unaware. Your ears and eyes get buried in a pussy and all you can hear is squish, squish, and all you can see is the black forest."

With every ounce of will in his body, he shook the woman off like a dog shaking off water. He crawled a few feet further and stopped. In front of him lay Abigail Robbins. The man was lying between her spread thighs, his face buried in her crotch while the woman held her legs up. Another woman was sucking gently on her right nipple. Robbins' body gave a little quiver from time to time. She was glistening with sweat. Her eyes were closed and she didn't see Christie. He didn't know what to do.

Finally he turned around and sat up with his arms outstretched behind him for support. He was breathing hard. The air was full of the odor of bodies and lovemaking, mixed with lingering smells of hashish and marijuana. He wondered if they had picked up Zachariah outside; he wondered how long this was going to last. Julia Preston had disappeared somewhere. He thought about grabbing Abbie and getting out, but maybe she wanted to stay. His senses were blurred. He looked up at the high priest and priestess. They remained standing above the burning altar; the priest's penis was still erect, and they were both shining with perspiration. Christie wondered at what point they joined the party.

The flute played on and the drums kept rapping out a frenzied beat. Christie brought his left arm in front of him. He looked at his watch. Twelve-twenty A.M. He brought his hand to his heaving chest and felt for the hanging amulet. It was gone.

From the farthest corner of the rectory basement, about twenty feet behind the altar, a pair of coal-black eyes burned through the darkness. Zachariah, God's Avenger, had sat patiently for five days, since Thursday, behind the wooden wall of the old coal bin near the interior staircase. He had witnessed the weekly Esbat Friday night in mute rage. He had been rewarded for his patience in waiting for the Sabbat. He almost bit through his lip as he stared into the circle of light. He had never seen or even imagined anything so unholy in his life.

He rose slowly and shouldered his big double-headed ax. No one noticed as he walked through the darkness and began mounting the ramp from the rear. The high priest and priestess heard the approaching footsteps but remained staring straight ahead. It was time for someone to escort them into the celebration below.

Christie was in a panic. He crawled desperately over the crowded floor looking for the leather pouch. He wondered again if Zachariah could actually give them the slip or overpower them and come crashing through the bolted door. Instinctively, he looked over his shoulder. His hands trembled as he furiously pushed through naked bodies looking for his gun.

Zachariah stood behind the goat-man and cat-woman, above the blazing altar. He raised the huge double-headed ax into the air. The heavy twelve-pound axhead hung suspended for a second.

Christie was almost at the base of the altar now, on his hands and knees. He caught a movement and looked up.

Zachariah brought the huge ax down directly between the horns of the goat head. Weirman's head split open like a melon. The ax fell with such force that it went through the neck and crushed the upper spinal column and breastbone. Blood and brains splattered over the cat-woman, and rained down on Christie's naked body. Weirman pitched forward and what was left of him fell between the ramp and the altar.

Zachariah swung the huge ax like a baseball bat and caught the high priestess squarely in the stomach as she turned toward him. The axhead opened her naked belly like a ripe tomato.

Someone behind Christie screamed. The music stopped. A silence filled the room as everyone stared up at the altar.

"I am Zachariah!" the huge monk screamed.

No shit, Christie thought wildly as he rubbed the brains and gore out of his eyes.

"Thou hast blasphemed the Lord God and thou shalt die for it!" he screeched. "Filthy and obscene demons!"

Zachariah leaped from the ramp and with one strong hand grabbed the chain from which the inverted cross hung. His feet hooked under the burning brazier on top of the altar and flipped it into the air as he swung forward. Burning jellied fuel, like napalm, scattered over the naked bodies on the floor. Complete panic cut loose. The jellied fuel clung, and burned the naked witches; the sweet smell of burning flesh and the acrid smell of burning hair hung over the room. Male and female screams cut through the air. A few remaining black candles provided a weak illumination, and in the darkness, bodies jumped around trying to brush off the burning fuel. The basement resembled a scene straight from hell.

Zachariah dropped from the chain and fell heavily on the naked chest of a girl who had passed out. Bones cracked. He stood erect and began swinging his ax with the precision of a helicopter blade. Round and round. The axhead and handle had picked up some of the burning fuel; it looked in the darkness like the burning sword of Judgment Day. The ax struck flesh and bone time and again. Zachariah laughed as he heard the sounds of a splitting head here, the crunch of bones there, the screams of his victims.

Christie dragged his burned body over to the spot where he last remembered seeing Abbie. Once or twice, a shower of warm liquids splattered over him. The wildest, most agonizing and heart-rending screams filled the room. Pleading voices shouted for mercy—for forgiveness. Some true believers and diehards shouted for Satan to rise up and destroy their torturer.

Christie heard a pitiful voice calling, "Peter, Peter." He crawled toward the voice of Abigail Robbins. She sounded hurt—wounded.

When the remaining candles had been toppled, the melee became even more confused. The napalmlike fuel died out; pitch darkness remained. The witches became confused in their drugged stupor. In the darkness they repeatedly lost their bearings, sometimes running into Zachariah, who immediately dispatched them to hell with his bloodred ax. Many of the survivors had instinctively headed for a wall after the last light had died away. They stood quaking with their backs against the dark cold stone. Except for the moans of the wounded, the cellar became strangely still. Christie could smell the stench of blood and open body cavities. He stifled a gag.

Every time Zachariah heard a moan he ran and buried his ax into the noise. Christie remained motionless on the floor. Zachariah's huge bloody foot walked across his back.

The big monk realized that his prey had scurried to the corners of the room, like rats. Methodically, he moved down the wall, swinging his ax in front of him. A few more witches died under his swift onslaught.

A dozen crying and screaming people had found the back cellar door. They pulled and fought with each other in pure panic. Many hands clawed and pulled at the door bolt. Finally, when it was thrown open, the crush against the door made it impossible to open it because it swung inward. The cooler heads tried to reason with the wilder ones to stand back, but they quickly lost control and began screaming and pushing.

Zachariah approached the noise at a run. They

could make out his huge bulk in the darkness as he drew nearer. The screaming became louder, shriller. The ax cut the air and severed an arm, then a leg. The survivors scattered. Zachariah stood at the door for a moment, then bolted it. The only way out now was up the interior staircase, but the door at the top of these stairs that led to the rectory was nailed shut. Zachariah knew it was nailed shut because he had nailed it himself after he'd gotten into the basement five days before. He paused now and listened.

Christie ran his hands over naked, limbless bodies. Quietly, he called, "Abbie."

No answer.

His hands found things he didn't want to think about. The floor was puddled with blood and liquid gore. Pieces of flesh lay everywhere. He felt a rising nausea, but fought it back. He groped around in the quiet dark, feeling for one or the other of the leather pouches. His burnt body was a mass of pure agony when he moved.

"Abbie," he whispered.

Zachariah approached.

Christie felt himself losing his grip. Tears filled his eyes. Then he heard it, a soft cry. "Peter."

Zachariah stumbled over a body as he ran toward Christie.

"Help me, Peter."

Zachariah was up in an instant. Like a bat, he had found the direction of Abigail Robbins' voice. He was coming for her.

Desperately, Christie screamed her name, trying to divert the mad monk from his bloody destination, but Zachariah was like the wrath of God. He could not be stopped.

"Peter," Abbie whispered, as the monk towered over her in the burning darkness. "Thank God."

"Witch!" Zachariah screamed, bringing the ax

down on her head with a two-handed horizontal stroke. The blade caught Robbins just above the eyes and sliced off the top of her head. Having nothing to hold them in, her eyes dribbled down her ruined cheeks. Zachariah screamed in triumph. Another witch had been saved.

"Abbie! Abbie!" Christie screamed, but he had heard the sickening sound of steel on bone. Zachariah was coming for him next.

Christie, the panic starting to take hold of him, scrambled to get away. His hands passed over a soft breast. It was warm, but very still. Then he caught the faint smell of herbs. He moved his hands from the breast and his fingers found the leather pouch. His heart racing, his hands trembling, he pulled at the snaps.

Zachariah took a long step forward and raised the ax.

Christie could smell the foul odor of the unwashed monk over everything else. With a calmness that surprised him, he pulled the small .25 automatic from the pouch, cocked it, aimed, and fired all seven rounds straight up into the hovering black figure.

The huge monk bellowed and dropped the ax. He reeled back and fell. Four of the small .25 rounds had buried themselves in his thick chest muscles. One round had passed through his forearm and the sixth had grazed the side of his broad temple. The seventh went wide.

Christie had no illusions about a .25 caliber round stopping a giant like this unless he hit him in the heart or brain. Even then, a .25 sometimes couldn't pass through so huge a man into those vital organs. The idea was to slow him down. Christie listened for a moment, then grabbed for the ax where he had heard it fall. His hand wrapped around the handle. A pull from the other end told him that Zachariah wanted the ax also. There was no use having a tug of war with this giant, wounded or not, Christie reasoned calmly. The ax handle slid out of his hand. He backed away.

He could hear shoulders crashing furiously against the solid oak outside door and also against the interior door at the top of the stairs. The screams and shots had alerted his back-up team.

He could hear Zachariah rise. Christie stood unsteadily. It was only him and the monk now. He dropped the useless gun. It rang out as it hit the floor. Zachariah swung. Christie ducked. The ax blade fanned his face.

The inside door at the top of the stairs began to splinter, but the outside door held firm. Zachariah let out a maniacal laugh. "You shall die, witch!" Christie's blood froze. He backed into an oak pillar. The ax swung. He fell to the floor. The huge ax crashed into the supporting pillar. Incredibly, the pillar cracked. The ceiling groaned overhead.

This bastard doesn't know he's been shot, Christie thought in amazement.

Zachariah pulled at the ax and drew it from the oak. In the split second it took to do this Christie leaped to his feet and sprinted toward the sounds coming through the outside door. Zachariah was after him in a flash. Christie misjudged the distance to the door and smashed into it. He was partially stunned; he felt his legs buckling. With clawing fingers, he raked the door until he found the bolt. He could hear Zachariah's wheezing breath close behind him. The cops on the other side were ramming the door furiously with their bodies, but Christie knew that they had little space to maneuver in the closed stairwell. Zachariah swung. Christie threw the bolt open and ducked. The ax crashed into the solid door. Christie rolled across the floor and stopped with his back against cold stone. He reached into the darkness. He was in a corner.

Zachariah turned toward the sound of Christie's labored breathing. The cops kept charging the unyielding door.

"The knob!" Christie yelled, near hysteria. "Turn the fucking knob! It's open!"

The door continued to reverberate with loud thumping sounds as Zachariah staggered toward Christie. The upstairs door was still creaking and popping but it held also. The monk raised the big ax.

"The knob! For God's sake, turn the knob!" Christie was beginning to give up. He sat back in the corner and waited. The monk laughed.

The pounding on the door stopped. Someone turned the knob. The door swung open.

Ryker stepped into the cellar. He was still dressed in a witch's robe.

"Zachariah!"

The big monk swung around. Moonlight cast a large rectangle of light where Ryker stood in the doorway. The monk began moving toward Ryker in a crouch.

Ryker raised his .357 Magnum and held it out with both hands. He could make out Christie directly behind the monk; he hesitated, fearing the bullet would pass through the monk and into Christie.

Zachariah charged like a wounded rhinoceros. In two big strides he was on top of Ryker. The big cop dropped to his knee and fired. The long gun bucked hard in his hands. The roar of the Magnum exploded in the closed room and died away in soft echoes. The monk stood still. He neither went forward nor backward. The bullet passed through Zachariah and splattered on the stone above Christie's head. Zachariah took a step forward. Ryker pulled back the heavy hammer and fired again. The monk staggered backward but kept his balance. Suddenly, he spun around and raised the ax above Christie's head. The ax hung for what seemed like an eternity. Then slowly, the monk sank to his knees not more than two feet from Christie. Both men looked into each other's eyes for a moment. "Sinner," Zachariah whispered hoarsely. "Die." The ax dropped from the monk's hands as he slumped forward and landed on Christie. Christie vomited onto the monk's black robe.

The banging on the upstairs door stopped and cops started pouring into the cellar from the open rear door. Ryker ran over and grabbed the monk's cowl and pulled backward. The huge body rolled off his partner.

The monk looked up at Ryker with haggard, red-rimmed, mad eyes. "For the love of God . . ." he gurgled, the blood pouring from his lips.

"Amen, motherfucker," Ryker said, firing a three-inch-long .357 shell into the monk's right eye. Zachariah's thick skull blew apart, sending bits of bone and diseased brain splattering around the room. Ryker watched the gore ooze down the wet stone wall, then he helped Christie to his feet. "She's dead," Christie said softly.

Ryker nodded. He looked at his watch. Twelve thirty-five A.M.

The whole massacre had taken less than fifteen minutes.

Christie stood burned and naked as the cops moved phantomlike into the darkness with powerful flashlights.

Christie's blood-splattered body shook with sobs as someone gently put a blanket around his shoulders.

Somewhere in the dark, a cop got sick. Another cop said, "Oh, my God . . . my God . . ."

EPILOGUE

When civilians are massacred and a cop dies in the line of duty, it's expedient to produce a scapegoat. Ryker was nominated. It was his operation, as Connolly was enjoying the hospitality of the asylum for the terminally inept. Departmental trial papers were drawn up, and everyone agreed it looked very bad for Sergeant Ryker this time.

Suddenly, though, a deputy police commissioner came to his defense. The DPC was unusually rigorous in his shielding of Ryker. A congresswoman joined forces on his side also. A few other prominent citizens offered their opinions to the police commissioner. Charges were quietly dropped. Everyone agreed that Sergeant Ryker had somehow latched onto powerful friends. He had political clout and leverage. When asked about it, Ryker only shrugged, his hard green eyes giving away nothing.

Abigail Robbins was buried with full inspector's honors at her family plot at St. Boniface Church in Elmont, Long Island. The full story of her death was never made public, but she was posthumously awarded the highest medal the NYPD could bestow. The police commissioner assured the parish priests that she had died in a state of grace and conditional absolution was granted according to the laws of the Catholic church.

Ryker and Christie arrived at the graveside services separately and they left separately. They exchanged no words.

Peter Christie's amulet was found around Julia Preston's neck. This looked bad for the young cop, but instead of a departmental trial, Christie was retired due to a medical disability. Some said Ryker had something to do with this.

The nature of Christie's disability was described as partial but permanent, brought on by traumatic shock. His burns were third-degree and would heal with scars, but the bad scars were the ones left on his mind by that nightmare in the Charles Street rectory basement.

Christie left the United States and took permanent residence in Israel, making the desert bloom.

A team of medical examiners, including Dr. Morlock, waded into the twenty-eight dead bodies strewn across the rectory basement. Forty-eight hours later, they had all the arms, heads, and legs where they belonged and wrote out twenty-eight certificates of death. Four more of Zachariah's victims died later in the hospital.

Zachariah, God's Avenger, remained a mystery. They never learned his real name or where he came from. When he failed to pay his weekly rent, the manager of the building opened his room, looked inside and called the police.

When the police arrived, they discovered nothing to identify Zachariah, except a faded photograph of a drab, gray-haired woman with a hard expression. His mother? His wife, girlfriend, sister? No one knew.

A letter was found, though, addressed to Brother Zachariah and postmarked Salem, Massachusetts. It read:

Brother Zachariah,
    The brothers send their blessings. Our glorious work continues. God has ordained that I, too, should begin my work in the wicked city where you now dwell. I will be arriving shortly. The council has decreed that our paths may never cross, but I will be working at your side in spirit. Death to the enemies of God.

                              Yours in vengeance,
                              Brother Jeremiah

Two weeks later, on June 21, the Festival of the Summer Solstice, a young waitress who worked in a saloon called Satan's Brew was found murdered in her apartment. There was a stake through her heart.

Joe Ryker didn't seem particularly interested in the case. "You read about one mad monk," he explained to the detectives near his desk, "you read about them all."